AEGEAN SUN:

The Market Place

Stephanie Wood

ISBN-13: 9798430283605

The Aegean Sun series of books:

CONTENTS

APRIL

The air around the church and down into the square was heavy with excitement and anticipation as a huge gathering of worshippers whispered greetings to each other and passed the flame from candle to candle in their traditional Easter midnight celebration.

The holy light from the altar had been passed from the priest to the congregation and they had spread it through the waiting crowd outside who were mesmerised by the vision of brightness which was gradually making its way down the street and into the hands of the town's faithful. Their challenge was now to take the candle home without losing the flame – not an easy task on such a windy night.

'Put your hand around the top to protect it, or it'll blow out,' Theo advised.

'But it's burning my fingers when I do that,' Selina replied, with an exasperated sigh.

'We should have got one of those plastic covers they were selling.'

'But you said it would probably melt into the wax,' she reminded him.

'Yeah, but it might have given us a bit more time. I don't think we're going to get home with them still intact,' he shrugged.

'Me neither, but,' she paused as she eased them both into a shop doorway, 'we might both live a little way from here, but we do spend an awful lot of time practically next door...'

'At the market?'

'Of course. We could take our candles there and draw the cross on that door instead of battling to get all the way home, where my parents will have taken theirs anyway. That way, we would have blessings at work as well as at home.'

'That's a good idea,' Theo said, considering the advantages. 'Also, we'd then be free to go for a drink at the harbour and enjoy the fireworks and celebrations.'

'Just what I was thinking,' she smirked as they hurried around the corner to the market place where a good deal of their time was spent manning their stalls.

Theo sold souvenirs of the island in many different forms: tea towels, fridge magnets, stationery, bottles, mugs, mouse mats, coasters, calendars and the obligatory ornaments of places of interest. There were other typically Greek ornaments he could probably have sold for the comedy effect, but he felt that their revealing nature belittled the professional atmosphere he was trying to create with his mini emporium.

Selina worked on her parents' stall, selling a variety of spices, honey and olive oil. She knew all the basic processing methods and the customers loved hearing about how each and every item was produced, before they bought as much as they could carry. When it was a holidaymaker buying all the goods, she wondered how they would fit everything into their suitcase, but never queried it at the point of sale in case they changed their minds.

When they got to the harbour, they ordered their drinks in their favourite bar and returned all the good wishes of future blessings while they enjoyed the usual traditional celebrations. There were fireworks over the castle, firecrackers in the street and indescribable explosions from the mountains above, which were echoed with equal ferocity from the hills of the neighbouring island.

In Greece, no celebration came anything close to the excitement enjoyed at Easter, but some of the early holidaymakers of the season were clearly shocked by the volume and chaos of the festival. They uttered a soft 'Aah' as they appreciated the display of fireworks, which was followed by a shrieked 'Eee' as a firecracker was released close to their feet. The inevitable 'Ooh' of nervousness was released when the mountainous blasts began, only to be diminished with a fearful 'Uuh' when the detonations across the water signalled their challenge for victory. The locals were never surprised when the unprepared tourists made an early night of it as the unusual festivities often seemed to be too much for them, but usually a good time was had by all and many memories were made, to be recalled and discussed through the generations at every family gathering.

Once the initial merriment and mayhem had settled, the conversation flowed a little easier.

'Did you hear my auntie's comments about us soon being together at the church again?' Selina asked.

'Yes, though my mum also made a sarcastic remark about me going there tonight. She said she thought I was avoiding making arrangements because I must be allergic to the incense, or the candle wax.'

'Hmm. Maybe you should have said it was true.'

'I just said I wasn't prepared to kiss the icon when half of the town has already slobbered all over it,' Theo grimaced. 'That much is true.'

'They're going to keep pushing though. Unless we're prepared to arrange a date for the wedding soon, we'll have to come up with an irrefutable reason why we're not ready yet.'

'But not being ready yet should be the only reason they need. We're not even ready to live together yet, so that should be enough for them. We've got a bit more life to live before we settle down and create their ancestors.'

'Which is all they really want,' Selina nodded.

'Just because we've been together since school doesn't mean we have to go any faster than anyone else. I keep telling them that there's only one of our friends who is already married and that was only because they got caught out...'

'With twins!' Selina finished with a laugh, before correcting herself. 'Although I shouldn't make fun of them if that's what's in line for me too.'

'I think it's probably likely that you and Leandra might end up with twins of your own, but maybe it could be a good thing to get it out of the way in one go, rather than go through the process twice, if you're planning on having two anyway.'

'Only a man could say that,' she grimaced. She had spoken to her identical twin sister Leandra many times about the idea of giving birth to twins and both had been very nervous about the possibility.

'What would I know?' he shrugged in apology, regretting his lack of compassion.

'Well, you know that neither of us are ready to take such a big step, so I'm really glad we're both on the same page.'

'But we always are; that's why we're so good together. We both want the same things.'

'Well, that's not exactly true,' she frowned. 'You want to spend the weekend playing poker with your mates and I want to go riding horses in the mountains.'

'But…'

'You want to watch Lip Synch Battle before bed and I want to listen to waterfall sounds.'

'I think…'

'You want to visit historical monuments and museums and I want to collect shells and pebbles on the beach.'

'It's just…'

'You want to have your own space to do the things you love and I want... the same,' she beamed.

'Oh, you're teasing,' he nodded. 'You got me.'

'And you've got me,' she said as she leaned in to give him a reassuring peck on the cheek.

'We might want to spend our time in different ways, but we both want each other to have that independence to be ourselves and that's why I said we want the same things,' Theo confirmed.

'And we also *don't* want the same things, like marriage,' she laughed and lifted her glass for him to tap in a toast of compatibility.

'Cheers to that. Why don't you stay over at mine tonight?' he suggested with a warm smile.

'You know why. I was supposed to take my candle home so they're expecting me. I can't come up with an excuse for why I suddenly stayed out all night when they know I was here with you.'

'But they want us to get married! Surely they know that you sometimes spend the night with me? They can't believe that these odd nights are sleepovers at your friends' houses,' he said with a shake of the head.

'I don't know, but that's what we say and it's generally accepted. I think they would be ashamed if I admitted I stay with you sometimes; it's just not what they would do.'

'That's because they weren't allowed to sleep together before marriage, so they just got wed as soon as possible so they could enjoy each other.'

'Euw. That's too much information for my brain to think about parents sleeping together. La La La,' she sang to herself with one finger in her ear. The other hand was still holding the glass, which was now pouring a large amount of wine into her mouth to erase the scene in her mind.

'Well, I've got a spare room, you could say you're sleeping in there? You do that anyway, sometimes, when you pretend I'm snoring.'

'You do snore! The noise can be worse than your neighbour's stupid rooster, after a few drinks.'

'Is that a few drinks for me or the rooster?'

'That should be funny, but I wouldn't be surprised if the rooster does get sozzled on occasion, judging by his owner's drunken behaviour.'

'Maybe he gets drunk to sleep through the animal's noisy morning chorus? I don't blame him actually; I definitely get a better rest when I've had a few the night before.'

'You can sleep through anything after a big night. I'm usually twiddling my thumbs until midday before you surface and then we've missed the whole morning,' she gently pouted.

'And that's why we don't live together. It's much more fun when we just have illicit assignations and you go scampering off back home before sunrise,' he smirked.

'I don't scamper. I sneak.'

'Do you think there's time for us to have a bit of fun at mine before you "sneak" back home afterwards?'

'I think if you get me another glass of wine, that could probably be arranged,' she nodded, handing him the empty glass.

The market was busy for a Wednesday morning and there were lots of deliveries of fresh produce to be sorted and displayed.

As usual, Kyriakos was one of the first to arrive and he quickly began to create a colourful presentation of the local fruit on offer, followed by Vitaly who competed with him to make an equally vibrant display of his vegetables. They enjoyed occasional challenges from each other to mark certain feast days and celebrations with their themed arrangements and they were both fierce competitors, but they also respected each other as colleagues so it was all achieved in a fun and friendly atmosphere.

Theo could begin a little later than the others as he didn't have fresh deliveries to oversee and that suited him very well. Once the season really got started, he would arrive at the same time as the other vendors, because there were always tourists who would make an early start and pop in on the way to the bus station; while they were buying apples or grapes for the journey, he could sometimes tempt them with a fan or a map to make their journey a little easier. If he had time, he would often ask where they were going and give them a couple of ideas of what they might want to look out for; he enjoyed helping others to get the most out of his island, but it meant that they remembered him and would sometimes return for their souvenirs before the end of their holiday.

When Theo entered the market, he could see some kind of gathering around Selina's stall, so he quickly checked in with the chief cashier to see if any of his items had been sold before his arrival (but he wasn't surprised to learn there hadn't been any) and then hurried over to the group to see what was happening.

'Stand back a little, Theo, or your trousers will get soaked,' Selina advised.

He could see a smashed vase and lots of water on the floor but his girlfriend seemed to have control of the situation.

'What happened?' he asked, as he stepped towards the adjacent flower stall and realised the incident was connected to the unusually sparse and untidy display.

'There's no sign of Old Mr Mylonas and some of his flower deliveries were wilting in the hall, so I tried to bring them in to get them on display but I didn't use a tall enough vase and the weight of the blooms tipped it over.'

'Has anyone called him?'

'Well he doesn't have a mobile phone, does he? Someone called the house but there was no answer so I think one of the delivery boys has gone over there to check.'

'What can I do to help?' Theo asked. He had no idea about flowers, but he could probably sweep up some broken glass. 'Shall I clear this up?'

'No, the caretaker's coming now with a mop so he'll take care of it. Can you bring in the rest of the delivery and I'll arrange it on the stall as best I can? If I spread it out a bit maybe no one will notice that it's a bit limp. Kyriakos is going to slice up some of the damaged fruit he can't use into a display to make the flowers look a bit more appealing until we can work out what's going on.'

'I hope he's alright. Old Mr Mylonas has been here for years and I've never known him to miss a day; this stall is his life.'

'I know. Everyone's worried, but I said he might have been called to his son's place in Athens for some reason, or maybe he decided to have a day off and forgot to arrange help here?' Selina offered hopefully.

'Unlikely,' Theo frowned. 'He's not the forgetful type.'

'But we have to stay positive. I couldn't bear to think something had happened to him,' she said through stiff lips which were threatening to collapse into a trembling mess.

Several of the vendors set about arranging the stall for Old Mr Mylonas and when it was finished they thanked each other with a degree of genuine affection, while keeping a larger supply in reserve for their friend and colleague who they hoped would be with them again very soon.

'Ah, here you are,' a familiar voice greeted Theo as he returned to his stall.

'Mark! It's great to see you back again,' he replied as he shook his friend's hand in greeting.

'Where else would I be? More to the point, who else would put up with me?' he laughed.

'You're always welcome here,' Theo assured him, glancing with interest at the young lady beside him.

'So, this is Rosie. Rosie, this is Theo. He is the owner of this fine souvenir emporium and, also, the best poker player I know!'

'Welcome Rosie,' Theo nodded in greeting. 'Are you a new rep working with Mark this year?'

'Oh, Rosie's been here a few years, although she's been living in Kefalos until recently, but she's come to work for us as a guide this summer, so you'll be seeing her regularly when she brings people here as part of the Kos Town tour.'

Rosie smiled somewhat timidly and it didn't seem that she really had the confidence to control an organised group of holidaymakers on a whistle-stop tour of the island.

'Is it your first time as a guide?' Theo asked, while trying not to notice how her blonde hair and nervous eyes reminded him of how Princess Diana used to look.

'Oh, no. I used to guide a few trips from Kefalos, around the south coast and the mountain villages so I'm used to showing people around, but I haven't worked in Kos Town before.'

Theo struggled to form a sentence as her light Irish lilt had surprised him, but he had to hear it again.

'You know, it won't take long to get used to Kos Town; I'm sure you'll settle in very quickly.'

'I'm living in Kardamena at the moment, because a friend of a friend is letting me stay with them while I, erm, get used to my new situation. I think I'll just settle into the new routine from there for now and enjoy this weekly trip before I decide if I'm going to make a more permanent move.'

'Well, you're very welcome here and I look forward to your weekly visit. Has Mark given you a sketch of the market layout?'

'Yes, I did,' Mark confirmed, as he waved a piece of paper in the air as evidence. 'We've just done a quick walk through of the best route and that's why we've finished up, as usual, with your stall. I've let Rosie know to guide the group to this spot and then let them fend for themselves, since we know they are more likely to be interested in the souvenirs initially, then they'll be more in the mood to mooch around for the local produce afterwards.'

'And then I just wait for them outside?' Rosie asked.

'Or you can just give them a time to meet at the steps of the museum opposite while you do your own thing,' Mark suggested.

'Actually, the guide last year used to sit here with me for a coffee while the group wandered around so you'd be welcome to do the same, if you wanted to,' Theo offered with a slight shrug.

'Oh, well, that's very kind,' Rosie smiled politely, but it didn't quite reach her eyes. 'Maybe it might be nice to stay inside under the air conditioning when the summer heat kicks in, but I'll probably need ice cream rather than a coffee.'

'We can do that too,' Theo nodded. 'What's your flavour? I'm a rum and raisin guy.'

'My default is chocolate, obviously. I mean, everyone loves chocolate, don't they? But I have been known on occasion to spice things up with banana, although I never usually eat the fruit itself. Weird, hey?'

'Not at all,' Theo laughed. 'I don't generally eat handfuls of raisins on their own either.' He was pleased that some of her nervousness seemed to have faded away and he was pleasantly surprised by her easy conversation.

'Well, I need to get back to the office to prepare some welcome packs,' Mark said. 'Are you going to hang around here Rosie, or will you be making your way back to Kardamena now?'

'I thought I might have a look inside the museum while I'm here and then get a drink in the harbour to soak up the atmosphere.'

'Sounds like my perfect kind of day,' Theo mused. 'Unfortunately, I have to stay here and look at the island's memorable places of interest through the medium of pictures on the coasters, or by imagining a very tiny version of myself sitting inside the clay windmills I'm selling.'

'It's a hard life, isn't it?' Mark said sarcastically.

'Oh, no, sorry. That came out wrong. What I was trying to express was that Rosie will be experiencing exactly the type of thing I would do if I had a spare couple of hours, so I just wanted to say she should make the most of it and enjoy each new experience to create a memorable moment; something she can remember in the future.'

'That's beautiful,' Rosie smiled. 'I definitely will try to do that. Thank you.'

'It's my pleasure,' Theo replied and meant it.

'See you soon, mate,' Mark called as he and Rosie made their way out.

As Mark turned right towards the office, Rosie looked over at the museum but, although she really did want to have a look around inside, she was still hanging on to Theo's words about making the most of things and registering each new experience and she knew she wouldn't be able to do that in public.

She followed the harbour road around to the end and strolled along the pathway next to the castle until she came out at the other side in a quieter area where there were a few benches overlooking the sea and out to Turkey in the distance. She slumped onto the bench and tried to catch her breath which had started to falter as she got closer to the place where she had chosen to examine her situation again.

Straight away, all the questions came flooding back and she had to concentrate to focus on them individually.

Why didn't I see what was happening?

Did I actually know that things were going wrong but somehow managed to hide it from myself?

Was I hiding the truth from myself because I was too scared to do anything about it?

Would I have been too scared to do anything about it?

Now that it's all out in the open, will I be too scared to go it alone?

What am I doing here?

Should I even have come in the first place?

Will I ever find someone who truly loves me for myself?

She didn't have the answers. She hadn't had them when things had been going wrong in her relationship and she didn't have them now that she had caught him in the middle of a passionate encounter in her own bed. In fact, she had even more questions now that she had fled the only home she had known for the last three years and moved to a completely new town where she knew nothing and no one.

She hadn't told anyone back in Ireland because they all thought she was mad in the first place to up sticks and go to live in Greece for what they'd openly said would be just a holiday romance. She had made sacrifices to keep her relationship going and it had been a huge challenge to pretend everything was going well when her partner had regularly found other ways to spend his time without inviting her along, or even letting her know where he was. She'd given up a lot to move to Greece but even she could now see that the initial passion which had instantly prompted her to change her life overnight, hadn't lasted more than one season. They got along well enough in the quiet winters to give her hope, but they hardly saw each other during the summertime and she could see, in hindsight, that it had been over long before it was officially over.

The problem now was hiding her hurt pride and working out, if she wasn't with the person she came to Kos for, how could she stay in Kos? She loved the island, but she had called Kefalos home and now she couldn't live there and risk constantly bumping into him, or any of their mutual friends who had always really been his friends anyway. She was trying to be realistic about the end of their relationship, but it still hurt that he had betrayed her in their own home and she was sure that vision wouldn't leave her mind for a long time.

And here were the tears again. She couldn't keep going over what had happened because her heart couldn't take the rejection and the tears seemed to fall whenever she struggled to be strong enough to see it for what it was. She had loved him, probably still did for now, but it was over and she was better off having a life of her own where she didn't need to keep pretending that everything was great. In the future she would no doubt meet someone who could make her feel special and loved, but she wasn't ready for that yet and had to work on herself first.

She had an image of Theo and his smiling eyes which had seemed to look right inside her soul. Maybe he could be the friend she needed to cheer her occasionally because she had been feeling very nervous about the new guiding job in unfamiliar surroundings, but he had made her feel comfortable and very welcome. Obviously, she wasn't looking for a new boyfriend and it was possible she might give up the job and go back to Ireland soon anyway, but in the meantime, it would be nice to have a new friend who she hadn't met through her ex, to enjoy a casual conversation now and again which would always be a pleasure.

She smiled to herself and felt confident that she would be able to make a new start with the Kos Town tour and was sure that she would enjoy every moment of it, however long it lasted.

Leandra rushed through the market place, giving Theo a cursory wave in her haste and headed straight for Selina's stall.

'So, where's this gorgeous new guy?' she asked, looking around impatiently while trying to catch her breath.

'Wow, word really does travel fast,' her sister replied. 'I'm guessing you mean Old Mr Mylonas' grandson?'

'Grandson? How old is he exactly?'

'I've no idea. I haven't spoken to him yet. Who told you he was here?'

'I was just getting my nails done and the girls were talking about him taking over from Old Mr Mylonas and how gorgeous he was. They were debating how often they could come in to get new flowers for their salon and who might get lucky with him.'

'Unbelievable!' Selina responded. 'The poor guy must be trying to come to terms with his granddad having a stroke and now he'll have to fend off random women with ulterior motives.'

'But the old man's fine, isn't he? They said he'll recover easily enough. Ooh, maybe this new guy is just here to help out for a few weeks until Mr M gets back on his feet, so he might be looking for a bit of fun after all,' Leandra smiled suggestively.

'Do you ever think of anything else?'

'Do we ever get gorgeous new talent to ogle at? No. To both questions.'

'Well, he's just gone with the caretaker to speak to one of the suppliers so he's not here to ogle at anyway,' Selina said sharply.

'What's his name?'

'I don't know,' Selina lied.

'Is he really gorgeous? Like, Keanu Reeves gorgeous?'

'I don't know, I only saw him from a distance. He looked OK.'

'OK? Do you even notice other men now you're due to walk down the aisle with good old Theo? Getting married shouldn't stop you from enjoying the view, if you know what I mean,' Leandra winked.

'I just haven't been introduced to him yet, so I don't know anything about him. I'll let you know if I get to meet him and find out what's going on with the stall. Now, if you don't mind, I've got work to do.'

'Yeah, I've got a shift at the cinema now, so I should be going anyway.' She checked her watch. 'Oh, I'm only ten minutes late, that's early for me!' she laughed as she hurried on her way.

Selina gazed at the departing vision of her sister with a mix of admiration and annoyance. Everything in her life appeared to be so easy and casual and she was always having fun, which the family allowed her to enjoy without any expectations or criticism. She, on the other hand, was constantly being hounded for a wedding date and hints about starting a family while she was still young, not to mention the snide comments that Theo would probably want to marry her much sooner if she wore more make up and dressed a bit more attractively. They meant if she looked more like Leandra.

Her sister was always made up as though she was ready for a photo shoot, with cat's eyes, plumped lips, hair straighter than a ruler and nails which looked like talons. Selina preferred the natural look and Theo had told her many times that she didn't need to wear a mask to look beautiful because she was absolutely perfect as she was. Of course, she made an effort for special occasions and for most of her dates with Theo, but it got really humid in the market so applying make up was pointless and dealing with foodstuffs all day would have been difficult with long nails, so when they would go out together after work she was quite casual, just adding a quick coat of lipstick and mascara to accentuate her best features.

Selina and Leandra were identical twins, born only a few minutes apart, but they were completely different in almost every aspect of their lives and depending on Selina's mood at any given time, that was either the best thing, or the worst thing ever.

She was momentarily distracted by a family who were interested in buying some honey but were confused about how it could have so many different flavours. She took pleasure in explaining that as there were many hives all over the island, each one was in a completely different habitat, so the bees would be visiting different flora in each area, resulting in individual tasting honey. The most popular and recognisable flavour was the thyme honey, which was pale in colour but still full of antibacterial and anti-inflammatory properties that could help to soothe colds and sore throats. The pine honey was a richer, amber colour and was created high in the mountain area where the bees fed on the sap of the trees rather than the flowers or nectar and it provided around 60% of all Greek honey. The smaller selection of jars in a darker brown shade was the fir honey and an acquired taste due to its mild nuttiness and slight sourness, which not everyone enjoyed, but many people used it for the prebiotic qualities. She mentioned the orange blossom honey, with the appropriate matching scent and colour which many customers asked for due to its light citrussy taste, but informed them that it was only readily available in western Greece and the Peloponnese.

The adults listened intently to her descriptions and advice, but they were all suddenly shocked into action when one of the children, who had been squabbling with his older brother, crashed down onto the bags of colourful spices after a forceful and authoritarian shove.

There was a lot of shouting and the children were grabbed by the shoulders and marched out of the market by their embarrassed parents who were alternatively angry and unsurprised.

Selina looked down at her display and was initially relieved that nothing had been broken, but as she began to tidy up the mess which had been created, she saw that one of the bags had actually split and the contents were beginning to spill out as she moved the other items around.

'Why does it have to be the saffron?' she moaned. Of all the herbs and spices she sold, the saffron was the most expensive so it was very bad luck that it had to be that particular bag which had burst.

'Need a hand?' someone asked and she smiled thankfully as she turned around, imagining Theo having run to her rescue.

'Oh! It's you!' she squeaked in surprise as the "gorgeous" new guy from the flower stall gazed back with a concerned expression.

'You've got something… on…' he muttered as he reached out towards her face, taking her by surprise.

'Ow,' she called as she fell backwards unexpectedly onto the hard wooden floor.

'Oh, I'm sorry, I didn't mean to scare you,' the new guy said in confusion. 'You just had something red on your face and I thought you might be bleeding.'

'Huh? I don't think so. Maybe you could help me up?' she suggested, finally managing to calm herself in front of her new work colleague.

She wiped her face with a tissue to remove the blob of saffron which had stuck there and wished her hair was less wild as she shook hands with her rescuer.

'I'm Selina. This is my stall, when children are not trying to destroy it.'

'Panos. I'm on the flowers.'

'Yes, I heard. You're Old Mr Mylonas' grandson, aren't you? How is he doing?'

'I am and he's doing fine. It's so funny to hear everyone call him that; I think this is the only place where I've heard that term, everywhere else he's just Mr Mylonas.'

'It's done in a friendly way; I think it was meant as a sign of respect somehow, but certainly no offence was intended.'

'And none was taken. He likes it; I think he believes it gives him gravitas and regard amongst his co-workers.'

'Co-workers? So he is coming back then?' Selina asked hopefully.

'Ah, that's a sore point, but I'm afraid he isn't. He would be back here tomorrow, but his doctor has advised him to take his long overdue retirement and the family is in agreement.'

'Oh, that must be hard for him to hear. He loved being around the market and in the midst of everything.'

'Yes, and he will come in to visit because nothing would be able to stop that, but his health isn't what it was and even though he should make a decent recovery, his working life has to be over now.'

'That will take some getting used to, from what I know of him. He always wanted to be involved with everything that was going on and the different celebrations and festivities that he would provide the most beautiful flower arrangements for.'

'Hmm, well that's where I have to step in now, although we all know I'll never be able to create the same kind of spectacular displays that he's been famous for. He will no doubt want to advise me, but we'll have to make sure there are boundaries in place so he doesn't get too involved.'

'Have you done this before then? Maybe helped him out with some of the regular events?'

'Nothing official, and certainly nothing recent. I used to enjoy helping him when I was younger and it felt quite natural with my creative personality, but I grew up and forged my own career and that took me away to the mainland so I didn't really have anything more to do with it.'

'Ah, yes, I know your father lives in Athens, so is that where you're based now?'

'Not a chance,' he laughed. 'When you get to know me, you'll understand why that's the last place I'd want to live. Even dad's not too keen on it, but he's a lawyer and that's where most of the decent work is, so he has to be based there for now.'

'Oh? You're not a fan of the city then?' She tried to ignore the way her throat involuntarily gulped when he suggested that she would be getting to know him.

'Not at all, although I do have to use the city connections from time to time for my work, but I do that in Thessaloniki and I live in the much more scenic area of nearby Halkidiki.'

'I've heard it's beautiful there, though I've never been. You don't have an office job then?' She knew she was being quite cheeky asking all the questions, but he did seem to be more than happy to discuss things with her. After all, if they were to get to know each other, they would have to understand the basics about their lives.

'No, I'm freelance. I work from home, or rather, in the surrounding regions and then confirm my projects, timescales and payments from a small rental unit in the city.'

'That sounds like quite the career. Will you have to leave it behind to work here instead? Surely you wouldn't give it up altogether?' She was desperate to know what kind of job he had as it sounded quite mysterious and exciting.

'No, I can do some work from here at the same time, but I won't be able to do that permanently. We haven't really worked out the details properly yet, but I think I'm just here to let granddad enjoy another year of the business without getting too involved, so he can get used to the fact that it's time to move on.'

'So will you be able to continue your job alongside creating the flower displays for the stall?'

'I hope so. In fact, it might be the ideal scenario to explore a new side to my portfolio. I usually concentrate on landscapes and the human form, but flora and fauna could be a new direction.'

'Which is…' her mind was reeling, but she thought she had a solution. 'Photography?'

'Close. I'm a freelance artist.'

'How wonderful!' Selina was in awe. 'It must be such a special gift to be able to improve what you can see in front of you, by bringing out the tiny details and the variety in the depths of colour in your own individual way.'

'It sounds like you understand why I love it so much,' he beamed.

'Of course. It must be a pleasure to be able to make a living from something you enjoy so much.'

'I'm very lucky that I found my dream and made it a reality.'

'Well, I hope you do get the opportunity to work while you're here. There are certainly many stunning things on this island which deserve to be shown to the rest of the world,' she gushed.

'I agree with you there. I've definitely seen some beautiful creations here which I would love to spend more time with, to understand them more deeply and to recreate their form in a special way,' Panos declared slowly and thoughtfully.

'Hi, Kyriakos told me you'd had a bit of a disaster here while I was on my break,' Theo said as he stepped in front of Selina.

'Erm, yes,' she stuttered, unsure if she was reading too much into what she had just heard from her new colleague. 'But I'm sorting it out.'

'I can give you a hand,' he offered as he glanced sideways at Selina's companion.

'Oh, this is Panos, he's looking after the flower stall for a while. This is…'

'I'm Theo, Selina's fiancé. I work on the souvenir stall,' Theo smiled tightly as he shook Panos' hand.

'It's nice to meet you,' Panos replied with a polite nod. 'Looks like your knight in shining armour has come to rescue you, so I'll get back to sorting the flowers,' he said in a friendly manner, but his quick exit was noticeable and awkward.

Theo and Selina quickly rearranged the messy shelves and rescued most of the saffron from the split bag as it had opened close to the top rather than anywhere lower down, making the spillage minimal and therefore not the disaster it may have been.

They made polite conversation, but Selina didn't reveal any of the conversation she'd had with Panos, as she felt that he'd opened up to her instinctively and it wouldn't feel quite as special if she repeated it to Theo, knowing he didn't have a very creative mind. She was slightly confused as to why he had introduced himself as her fiancé, when that word hadn't been used outside the family, but as it was unofficially the truth, she had no cause to question him.

At the end of the day, Selina and Theo enjoyed a tasty gyros from the fast-food restaurant on the corner of the square and then picked up some chocolate to take to the cinema, where Leandra had obtained some free vouchers which they could use for that night's showing. No one asked where the vouchers had come from because they didn't want Leandra to have to lie, but they really wanted to see the movie so they made good use of their connections for a fun evening.

MAY

Rosie halted her line of guests in front of the souvenirs, but hesitated when she couldn't see Theo in the nearby area as she had planned to introduce him so that he could point out a few of the best items.

'You might recognise this gorgeous little windmill,' she began, picking up the small ornament, 'from our visit to Antimachia this morning.' She inspected the faces of her audience and was pleased to see some recognition in most of their expressions, so she hoped it meant that she had succeeded in keeping them interested and involved.

'Where are the statues of the big Greek blokes?' one of her guests asked with a huge grin. 'You know the ones I mean; the hunky ones with the huge...'

'I don't have any statues of hunky blokes,' Theo interrupted as he returned from a call of nature, 'but will I do?' he winked.

'Oh, yes,' the woman blushed. 'You would definitely do. Ow!'

Theo presumed she hadn't expected to be nudged in the ribs by her husband who wasn't smiling quite as much as his wife.

'There are lots of other souvenir shops up in the Old Town on the other side of the square, which sell everything you could possibly imagine...' he hesitated, to allow the customers to understand what he was implying. 'Here, I have a sample of the finest and most popular souvenirs which I believe will give you the best memories of Kos itself and help you to remember the island and its residents long after you arrive back home.'

'So, I'll let you have a look around for yourselves and then I'll meet you in front of the museum at 3.30 for our journey back,' Rosie instructed as she casually moved towards the staff area to avoid the countless questions about what she thought they should buy.

She took out her bottled water and took a long gulp. The day seemed to have gone to plan and she had kept everyone busy on their dedicated pit-stops for amazing views, photo opportunities, historical trivia, natural life observations and shopping must-haves. There was a quick-fire quiz to look forward to on the coach as they headed out of Kos Town, with three prizes of honey, olive oil and a traditional Greek 'eye' keyring to be given to the first three correct respondents, but then she would switch off the microphone and relax for the rest of the journey until she dropped everyone off at their hotels. Hopefully by then they would be so pleased with their day that they would hand her some kind of tip which would supplement her guiding fee and make the expense of living alone a bit easier to deal with.

After a little while, Theo had finished serving the customers who'd stayed to buy a few souvenirs and he joined Rosie in the staff area, where he was still able to keep an eye on his stall in case anyone else approached.

'Sorry I was AWOL when you arrived,' he frowned. 'I wanted to be there to support you on your first visit.'

'It's fine,' she shrugged. 'It wasn't as tricky as I thought and luckily I remembered some of the things you'd told me about the different ornaments.'

'Still, I'd like to be ready next time you come. Give me your phone.'

'Er, what?' she panicked as she gripped her phone inside her pocket.

'Your phone,' he demanded, as he held out his hand.

'Why do you need my phone?' she asked as calmly as she could.

'So that I can give you my number. Then, next week, you can call or text to say that you're about to arrive and I can be ready to greet everyone.'

'Oh, right. I see,' she exhaled heavily. 'Just a sec...' She took out her phone and opened the contacts screen so that he could enter his details directly.

'There... you... go...' Theo said as he entered the last three digits. 'And now, I have your number too,' he added needlessly, as his phone rang in response to his speedy actions.

'Thank you,' she replied as she snatched back the phone before he could close the menu and return to the screen saver.

'So, have you got time for some ice cream, like we discussed?' he smiled cheekily.

'Oh, that would be nice, but where do we get it from?' she queried as she looked around for somewhere to relax.

'Only the best shop on the island! It's on the corner of the square so we won't be too far away and you'll be able to see your guests gathering when it's time to go.'

'Are you allowed to just leave your stall?'

'Well, it's my stall so I can do what I want! Anyway, I'm due a proper break and the general cashier at the entrance takes any transactions for the unmanned stalls, so no one loses out.'

'Right. Well, that seems like a good idea then,' she smiled eagerly.

'Hey, Li! You coming for some ice cream?' He shouted over to the spice stall, but received a quick shake of the head and a point to the adjacent stall.

'She looks busy,' Rosie offered. 'Is she a friend of yours?'

'That's Selina, my girlfriend. She's covering the flower stall as well today because the guy who's just taken over had to be somewhere else, for some unknown reason.'

'Oh, well, she's kind to do that for him. She must be a very generous person, your girlfriend.'

'Yes, too much sometimes, but she won't be told. Anyway,' he shrugged, as though to shake off a stray emotion, 'let's get that ice cream.'

They sat quietly for a moment, enjoying the sweet taste of their treat while being entertained by a few children on the square attempting to do tricks on their bicycles, though most of them weren't very successful.

'So, your girlfriend is called Selina?' Rosie asked cautiously, receiving a nod in response as Theo's mouth was completely full and he wasn't prepared to terminate his pleasure by swallowing quickly to utter one word of confirmation. 'But you called her something else? Leigh?'

'Mmm,' he groaned in reply as he lifted his finger to indicate that he would respond verbally in the time it took to get every last ounce of pleasure from the melting delight inside his mouth. 'Sorry, but that is just the best taste ever,' he drooled.

'Yeah, I should know better than to interrupt a man and his food,' she said, too quickly to hide her instinctive reaction, but hopeful that he hadn't really noted the sadness in her comment.

'Selina has a sister called Leandra and when they went to school together, she shortened it because they liked to be called Lina and Leandra, a pair who went everywhere and did everything together. Between themselves they shortened it even further to Li and Lea but as they grew up, they reverted to their full names again.'

'So you call her Li because... she wants to pretend she's a child again?' Rosie mused with slight distaste.

'No way,' he laughed. 'It's just that we met at school and became good friends immediately, long before we ever dated, so I got to know her as Li back then and now I'm the only one who uses it, so she likes having a special name.'

'Oh, I see. That's romantic,' she nodded with more enthusiasm than she felt. It would have been nice if someone had ever had a special name for her.

'Is it? It's just what I call her and she likes it; I never really thought of the romantic undertones,' he pondered.

'Well, hopefully you still think of the romantic undertones when it matters,' she nudged him with a smile, then realised it might seem a bit forward for such a new acquaintance.

'We don't really do romance any more,' he shrugged without hesitance or regret. We've been together nearly ten years now, so it's a bit late for all that.'

'Wow, that's a long time. You must have got together really young.'

'Like I said, we met at school and just hung out together all the time, but when school came to an end, we kind of decided we didn't want to part and so we officially became girlfriend and boyfriend from then on.'

'And you're still girlfriend and boyfriend?'

'All the way!' he smiled contentedly.

'No, I mean you're *still* girlfriend and boyfriend? Isn't she expecting you to propose by now?' Rosie asked in surprise and in support of a fellow woman who seemed to be waiting in vain.

'Well...'

'I'm sorry, that was so rude. And personal. And wrong. Forget I asked, it's none of my business.'

'Don't worry, you're not the first to ask and you won't be the last. It's not exactly private because everyone knows we're just happy to keep things as they are for now. We still feel too young to settle down and think about raising a family yet, but it's difficult to justify that to our families when they are constantly hounding us to give them a date for the wedding.'

'They probably just see a couple in love and wonder why you wouldn't want to commit to being together when you obviously care so much. You were lucky to find each other so early; some people go through a lot of false starts before they finally find the one.' Rosie was trying to sound supportive, but her comments were making her eyes water and that was not acceptable while sitting outside on such a sunny and beautiful day. 'But I'm sure they'll be happy to help you to arrange everything once you're ready for the next step,' she finished brightly.

'You'd better believe it. My mother has a folder with everything already planned out and Selina's mum has a duplicate with the added section of preferable wedding dresses. Whenever we give the word, it will probably be arranged within the week,' he laughed lightly. 'Although we haven't yet told them that we're not making any decisions until we're thirty, which is another few years, so that won't go down very well when they do demand some kind of date.'

'No, I can imagine your mum would be really looking forward to seeing you walk down the aisle and move forward with the next stage of your life. It's every parent's dream.'

'I know, but that's all they ever talk about – the wedding. Well, that and how many children we'll have. No one talks about the marriage itself and the years and years of opportunities we'll lose by settling down, or the lack of money we'll have to put up with when rent and repairs and kid's necessities take away any chance of travel and personal achievements. We can do anything we want to right now but no one seems to understand that we're not quite ready to give it up just yet.'

'I suppose they just grew up in a different generation, when personal achievements and travel weren't as important as having a family and continuing the traditions handed down to them. My own parents are similar and couldn't understand why I would move to Greece when they thought I should just get an office job and a rented flat in the same town as them. Things have really changed for everyone in the 21st century and the gap between the generations is wider than ever now.'

'You're right,' he agreed with respect. 'You've really hit the nail on the head and I'm not sure I've ever heard anyone explain it so clearly before. We've just been moaning to each other that our parents don't understand us and they have probably been thinking that we don't understand them. I might have another think about how to talk to them regarding our future plans, or current lack of them,' he grinned broadly. His face seemed to shine with the realisation that there could be another way of reaching some kind of agreement on the subject, for which all concerned would be happier and wiser.

'I'm glad if I helped,' she replied, warming to the conversation.

'Looks like your gang are gathering,' Theo pointed over to the museum where many of her guests were standing and looking around disconsolately.

'Oh, is that the time?' she asked in surprise, checking her watch.

'Afraid so. What do they say? Back to the chain gang, or something like that,' he suggested, raising his eyebrows. 'I guess we'd better get back to it.'

'I've still got a few minutes, so I'll nip to the toilet and pay for these ice creams,' she offered.

'No, it was my suggestion, I should pay,' he remonstrated.

'But I want to say thank you for welcoming me and helping me out on my first day. I insist.'

'Well, I do like a woman who knows her own mind. Thank you. The next one's on me,' he called over his shoulder as he made his way back to the market place.

Rosie was glad that he didn't see her blush as she luxuriated in his comment. She wasn't sure if it was because he had recognised and accepted that she was able to make her own decisions, or if it was the fact that he'd said he liked a woman like her. She hadn't even registered the fact that he had hinted at the possibility of this happening again, but when she did it made her blush even harder.

Once she had collected her group and dispensed with the gifts for the winners of the mini quiz, she relaxed in her seat and thought about what a lovely day she'd had. They had visited many different sights around the island, but somehow all she could think about was sitting in the square and enjoying ice cream with a lovely man who seemed to enjoy talking to her and that hadn't happened for a long time.

Her phone buzzed and she switched it on to see she had a message from someone called Hunky Greek Guy. She was momentarily confused, but thought it was fitting to be printed over the top of her screen saver which was a photo she had taken when doing her initiation around the market place. It was especially beautiful because she had zoomed in on one particular person who definitely stood out in a crowd – the same person who had made her feel so wonderful only a short time earlier. Obviously, she couldn't let Theo see an image of himself as her screensaver and she'd had to think quickly to avoid an embarrassing situation, but she smiled to herself as she realised the message was from him and understood that he had unwittingly given himself the most appropriate name, at the instigation of her guest's suggestive comment about the Greek statues.

THANKS FOR TODAY. I ENJOYED OUR CHAT. LET'S MAKE IT A REGULAR THING AND SOLVE EVERYONE'S PROBLEMS. LOL.

She held her fingers over the LOL as though it was a kiss and then quickly replied.

I ENJOYED IT TOO. IT'S A DATE.

She frowned to herself and deleted the last sentence.

I ENJOYED IT TOO. HOPEFULLY SELINA CAN JOIN US NEXT TIME AND WE CAN

DISCUSS YOUR STRANGE TASTE IN ICE CREAM... LOL.

She wasn't a fool. She recognised that she was madly attracted to Theo, but he had a (very!) long-standing girlfriend and she was not going to interfere with that. She was still nursing her hurt pride and her heart hadn't yet fully recovered, so she wasn't even ready to start thinking about a new relationship anyway. The fact was that she was lonely and without friends as she had moved away from everything she had come to know. What was the harm in getting to know some new people and maybe forming some new friendships along the way? And if they included a Hunky Greek Guy who was easy on the eye and made her pulse run a little bit faster, as long as she stuck to the rule of "look but don't touch" she decided she would be absolutely fine.

The sunglasses were taking the intensity out of the sunshine, but Theo was still having difficulty driving in the bright light which seemed to be reflecting off every known surface and making his head hurt even more.

'Ugh, why can't it have been a cloudy day today?' he mumbled.

'Because then it wouldn't have been fair on the rest of the family. Who wants to celebrate a christening on a cloudy day?'

'Who plans a christening this early on a Sunday morning?' he complained, he felt, justifiably.

'Who stays out until 4am getting drunk the night before an early morning ceremony?' Selina asked, equally justifiably.

'Will you stop answering my questions with more questions?'

'Will you stop asking such pointless questions?'

'I don't understand. I've stayed out later sometimes and not felt as rough as this. I'm glad I brought some spare painkillers; I'm going to need them today.'

'Well, you don't usually get up this early on your day off and, to be fair, I think it was probably switching to cocktails that did the damage.'

'How did you know about that?' he asked with a frown.

'You took selfies of you and Kyriakos and posted them all over your page. It definitely looked like you were having fun, but I was surprised to see you with a Pina Colada,' she smirked.

'That's because I refused to have some of the ones he was ordering; you know, those with the dodgy names.'

'I can imagine.'

'I don't think you can. That sweet, kind and gentle man turned into someone I didn't recognise when I refused one of the drinks he had bought as he went on to offer a free orgasm to anyone who would dance with him.'

'No way! Kyriakos? I can't picture that at all. He's usually so quiet.'

'I know. He got drunk really quickly, but then, so did I.'

'Well, you'd better put your game face on, or your mother will disown you.'

'Can we just drive down to the beach and make a quick stop first? I need to catch my breath.'

'There isn't time, but pull over at this kiosk and I'll get some water because I think you're going to need it.'

Selina got three small bottles of water, knowing that Theo would drink the first in one single action, leaving one for each of them to keep handy during the service.

A little further along the road, they entered the main street of Zipari and pulled up outside the Parish Church of the Ascension of the Saviour, a magnificent building which many visitors made a point of visiting for its architectural beauty. The small village, just a short ride from the main town, was growing in popularity amongst the locals as a more financially desirable place to live, with the added incentive of having a sandy beach easily accessible along the outskirts.

The couple greeted the immediate family of the tiny girl who was being baptised, a distant relative of Theo's, and then made their way into the church. His mother waved to them and indicated where they should sit, thankfully not right next to his parents, so there would be no opportunity to start off with an admonishment for the alcoholic fumes still surrounding him, even after a very lengthy shower and gallons of mouthwash.

There were many groups of friends present inside the church, as was usual with Greek celebrations, and it was perfectly normal for Selina's parents to have also been invited, as most of the group considered them to be family by now anyway.

Everyone was dressed as though they were attending a wedding, with sparkly dresses and huge hats which occasionally hindered the view of the action, but they were all glad to make an effort and mark the special occasion when baby Sophia was welcomed into church.

The ceremony began and everyone smiled as little Sophia screamed her lungs out after being immersed three times in the baptismal font. She was then handed to her godparent, who Theo recognised as the father's best man, who wrapped her in a white towel while she received the sacrament. Then she was dressed in the sweetest lacy white gown and the candles were lit, so that the necessary procession could be made around the font three times.

Theo was glad he hadn't been asked to be a godparent. Apart from the fact that he wasn't ready for the responsibility, he wasn't sure he would have been able to walk in such a tight circle without either falling over or, even worse, throwing up in front of all his relatives.

The priest concluded the service with a reading and everyone exited the church to begin the real celebration, which was far noisier and unrestrained than the fairly sombre affair they had just experienced.

The family house was just two streets away, so everyone walked there as they chatted and laughed and enjoyed the wonderful sunshine which was putting smiles on everyone's faces. Well, most people's faces.

'You smell like a brewery. How could you step inside church like that?' Theo's mother asked.

'I had a shower and put some good aftershave on,' he explained as he appealed to her better nature. It seemed she didn't have one.

'And that just makes it worse. Lucky for me, I know what the scent you use smells like, so I can recognise both aromas separately, but most of these other people will just recognise some zesty hints with undertones of garbage. You smell like rotten fruit!' she exclaimed with an expression which reminded Theo of someone sucking lemons. Quite apt, really.

'Well, there's nothing I can do about it now. It's better that I came, even in this unforgiveable state, than if I missed the whole thing altogether.' He knew that wouldn't have been an option, but it was all he had as an excuse.

'Just make sure you stay outside in the garden. It will be a hundred times worse if you stay indoors and poison everyone,' she huffed, as she increased her pace to evade his apparent stench.

'Looks like you'll have to be my waitress today, if I'm not allowed in the house,' he said to Selina, who had kept out of the parental altercation. She'd learned to stay out of any disagreements between mother and son because there could never be any winners and as long as she hadn't raised her point of view, she would be faultless when the debate was restarted - which it often was.

'Well, you won't be able to drink if you're driving, so you'll probably be bored after you've had some of the cake and I can relax with you instead of running round fetching and carrying.'

'Go on,' he smiled.

'What?'

'Finish the sentence.'

'I don't know what you mean,' she pouted, even though she had an idea what was coming.

'Like usual, you wanted to say.'

'Well, it does seem to be me who usually ends up helping out at this kind of event,' she admitted.

'That's because, one, you can never say no and two, you love helping people out and they all know it,' he said with a nod to the crowd which was assembling in the garden.

'There's nothing wrong with that.'

'No, but when you do it all the time, it's harder to get away when you just want to take it easy for a while.'

'I'm my own worst enemy, aren't I?' she smiled, enjoying the fact that Theo's light teasing was only because he knew her so well and loved how she was always ready to help whoever needed it.

'Well, you haven't got any other enemies, so that's not too bad a deal,' he confirmed as he gently lifted her chin with his fingers and placed a soft kiss on her lips.

'So you can carry on in public, but you're too ashamed to walk her down the aisle?' his mother said as she returned with a knife.

'Woah! What's that for?' Theo jumped back, wondering how the constant lack of wedding planning had suddenly turned into a vicious attack.

'It's for Selina,' she replied calmly, oblivious to his irrational fear. 'You need to help with cutting the cake,' she said as she handed over the knife which, at a second glance wasn't even sharp enough to dissect a crusty loaf. 'They're waiting for you, hurry,' she continued as Selina didn't move immediately.

'I'll get on with it then,' Selina said as she raised her eyebrows, but they both knew she was happy to be useful.

'Just as well I got here before you started kissing in public,' his mother muttered. 'You can't carry on like that in front of everybody when you haven't set a date for the wedding. Your father and I have been talking and we have to make some arrangements. Soon. The poor girl will be getting a name for herself and you will be seen as the one taking advantage. It can't go on Theofilos.'

'Mama, we're just not ready. We're still young with things we want to do before we settle down with financial commitments, let alone thinking about starting a family of our own.'

'But you can't just carry on being… casual,' she said with obvious distaste. 'Her parents must think we're so disrespectful, to treat her that way.'

'She's explained the same thing to them. They understand how we feel for now.'

'They understand? How can they understand? We've had many conversations with them and they want the same thing too. What are you waiting for? We all want to organise the wedding and see you married and settled.'

'But that's the problem. You want to see us settled and we're not prepared to settle for anything other than what we want, which is to wait to get married.'

'You're playing with my words now. Don't you want to be settled with a beautiful woman, and happy?'

'I'm already with a beautiful woman and happy. Why do I need to settle? When we're ready to get married, we'll do it, but for now we want to enjoy all the things which we won't have time or money for once we make that commitment.'

'What else can you possibly want to do now, that you can't do when you're married? In my experience it has been a blessing to have a husband by my side who I trust implicitly and to share all of life's pleasures as the years pass, including building a home together and welcoming the next generation. What else could be more important?'

'I don't think I can explain it properly,' he shrugged. 'Can't you just accept that we're not ready yet? It won't be forever.'

Theo was relieved when an aunt interrupted to ask for assistance from his mother. Yiayia wanted to speak to them about something and she couldn't wait. He believed that the only person who was more demanding than his mother was his grandmother, and he could recognise how her analytical character was no doubt genetic.

He really wished he could have a beer, though he needed something much stronger. Their frequent conversations about organising the wedding were just getting too much to bear. He couldn't find a way to explain why he just wanted things to continue as they were for the moment, because he was sure they wouldn't understand that he didn't want to give up his poker nights, or the possibility of costly international travel, or the ability to enjoy spontaneous and unexpected celebrations like the one he had suddenly been invited to the previous evening. On second thoughts, he could probably have missed that one without too much regret.

Clearly, he would still be able to have nights out and holidays once he was married. He and Selina were happy to let each other have individual interests as they both liked to do things independently, but there was more expectation to do things together and to put money towards mutual concerns once the vows had been exchanged, so that any personal pastimes would take on the need for justification and explanation, which would just make things awkward.

That was all it was, awkwardness. It just wouldn't be as easy-going and acceptable as it was now and that was impossible to explain to his parents. It was hard enough for him to admit it to himself because it was such a small argument, but he could see that it would completely change how he lived his life and he definitely didn't want that. He didn't want there to be any awkwardness between himself and Selina, over how they spent their time and money, when things worked so well for them at the moment. They each had their own space within their relationship and he really didn't want it to change at all, but marriage would do that and he had to put it off until they were both ready to accept a different way of life.

Selina returned with a tray offering a slice of cake and a small beer for each of them.

'That's just what I need,' Theo gasped as he grabbed the glass. 'Is it OK?' he asked, knowing that he couldn't resist, but worried about their no drink driving agreement.

'It's shandy, so yeah, I think you're OK with that,' she smiled.

'Hmm,' he murmured as he tipped half of the glass's contents into his mouth. He needed something strong, but the lightness allowed him to drink more quickly and it was truly refreshing.

'I take it your mother had more to say about the way you smell,' she giggled, seeing his need for replenishment.

'If only. It was the wedding story again. Apparently, you'll be getting a name for yourself by kissing me in public when I'm not making any effort to propose to you.'

'Seriously? What would she say if she knew about the times we…'

'Yiayia!' Theo called as his grandmother approached, hoping she hadn't caught any of Selina's words.

There was a quick rearrangement of the furniture so that the old lady could sit comfortably and it was only then that Theo and Selina realised both of their parents were standing behind her.

'Are you well, Yiayia?' he asked with concern. 'Do you need a drink?'

'I am perfectly well,' she replied impatiently, then directed her daughter to speak.

'Mama has just been speaking with her friend who is selling her house here in Zipari, so that she can downsize and move in with her family. It's a beautiful family home and would be ideal for a young couple to take on and make their own for the future.'

'Ah,' Theo exhaled. He had a good idea where this conversation was headed, but daren't look at Selina in case their expressions soured the mood.

'We think this is too good an opportunity to miss so Mama has agreed that she will pay the deposit and then make the repayments to the bank for a year while you build and decorate in a way you feel appropriate, so that it will be ready for you to move into after the wedding. It will be her gift to you as something to remember her by as you grow old there yourselves.'

'Right. That is so kind Yiayia,' Theo began, having no clue how to continue in order for them to understand that it couldn't happen. How could he vocalise his refusal without offending, or hurting, his beloved grandmother?

'It is exceptionally kind,' his mother stated with a warning tone. 'I'm not personally convinced you deserve that amount of kindness, but maybe you can put that right by making it a perfect family home in time for the wedding which we can announce today.'

'What? No! Sorry Mama, sorry Yiayia. This is all too sudden. It's a wonderful idea but we are really not ready to decide a wedding date yet and I can say with one hundred percent certainty that it will not be as soon as one year. Your gift is extraordinary Yiayia and I love you dearly, but we haven't decided where we want to live in the coming years, so can we just wind back five minutes and start again? I'm sure your friend will have lots of generous offers for her house, but it shouldn't be coming from you. We need to make our own decision about where we want to live and when we'll be ready to move there. Selina?'

'This is an unbelievable offer, Selina,' her father stated without expression. It was always difficult to see what was going through his mind and he wasn't giving anything away in that tense atmosphere.

'It truly is very generous,' she nodded. 'But it's really too much. I wouldn't feel comfortable accepting something so huge when I'm not sure it's what I really want. Also, if you don't mind me being honest, I would get much more satisfaction out of the challenge we would face in creating a place to live ourselves, remembering all the effort it took to save and work for everything we had made together. Does that make sense?'

'I think so,' her mother replied with a knowing smile. 'That definitely sounds like the kind of thing you would be good at.'

'But that still leaves us up in the air about when this wedding will actually take place,' Theo's mother cut in to puncture any possibility of an acceptable refusal. 'It's not dignified to be attending these celebrations together year after year, without an understanding of when you will finally make an official commitment to each other. We need a date.'

'We haven't decided yet, Mama. You know that.'

'So when will you decide? This year? Next year? In ten years? I could be dead by then.'

Theo could always rely on his mother to cause a scene and play her woe-is-me card to get attention. He was surprised that he hadn't realised his grandmother was the same, until she nodded her head and expressively folded her arms in a questioning show of support for her daughter.

'Not this year. Probably not next year. I would say definitely not before I'm thirty, if that helps,' he answered automatically with a shrug. It was something they had decided to reveal at some point, but he had expected it to be in a more private situation.

'But that's three years!' his mother exclaimed, raising her hands in the air. 'How can we wait that long?'

'I suppose you'll have to try,' he grimaced, wondering if that would get them all off his back and leave him in peace for a while.

'So, if we try, we can start to plan things to happen in three years?' she asked, calming a little as the ideas started to roll around in her mind.

'Well, I didn't exactly…'

'Good!' she interrupted. 'Well, at least that's settled. The wedding will be in three years, so we can start to plan which would be the best time of year and then get a venue booked. At least we will have a good choice with this much notice. Actually, maybe we should put a deposit on a couple of different places because anything could happen within that time and we don't want to be caught out at the last minute. Come,' she waved towards Selina's parents, 'we have lots to discuss.'

Yiayia and the parents all disappeared inside the house leaving Theo and Selina standing in the garden in complete shock.

'What just happened?' Theo asked, his mouth suddenly as dry as a bone.

'Your mother,' Selina replied with equal disbelief.

'I need to go and drive a fast jet-ski halfway to Turkey,' he said, as a vein throbbed viciously in his neck.

'I need to pound the surf on a jet-black stallion,' she countered breathlessly.

'I'll drop you off at the stables,' he nodded, as they turned and almost ran out of the garden towards their individual panic-soothing remedies.

Panos arranged an exquisite group of blood-red roses into a tall white vase and placed them at the top of his display.

'Perfect,' Kyriakos said as he held his hand over his heart. They were to have a similar effect on most of the people visiting the market that day.

'Now I just need to dress up the gaps with some of your tasty fruit, to entice the shoppers my way,' Panos pondered.

'What do you think will fit best?'

'Well, I want something that will gel with the colours I've already used so that it complements the flowers rather than distracts attention with too much garishness.'

'Garish? Moi?' Kyriakos replied with a laugh, as he brushed down the sleeves of his orange shirt.

'Not you, the fruit, but actually, yes, oranges would clash with the colour scheme. Maybe lemons would work though.'

'Yes, lemons would highlight the sharpness in the reds and pinks, but you need something with a bit more pizazz. Ooh, I know. What about a pineapple?'

'Hmm. That might work. The pointed edges would emphasise the soft curves of the petals, but I'm not sure if it would be too overpowering,' Panos mused.

'I'll bring one over. Maybe we could leave the top on display as a spiky contrast to the gentle flowers and then slice the rest of it up to tempt people with the smell? The customers could taste small pieces as they shop and it might encourage them over to my stall to buy something too.'

'That's probably a bit more than we need for now. Let's just see what a pineapple and a few lemons look like first. Here, while you're going, take these two posies over to brighten up your area, like we agreed.' Panos handed over the small flower sprays to Kyriakos who beamed his delight and ran back to his stall to arrange them appropriately.

The combination of flowers and fruit on each of their stalls had increased interest from the customers and they decided to make it a regular thing, although the constant change in colour availability created a new challenge every day.

The finished product looked very enticing and Panos was pleased with the effect, except for a couple of small areas which weren't big enough for additional fruit, but somehow seemed to lack a spark of something which he couldn't define. He gazed at the arrangement, but simply couldn't work out what was missing.

'Having trouble?' Selina asked as her customers departed.

'I'm not sure. Come and have a look,' he suggested.

She stood beside him and luxuriated in the beauty of the combination of red and pink, highlighted by the hue and scent of the lemons, with a solid centrepiece of a sturdy pineapple which gave an underlying strength to the delicacy of the entire display.

'It's beautiful,' she confirmed. 'Old Mr Mylonas used to create some wonderful displays, but this is really different. He must be very proud of you.'

'Well, he hasn't been in yet, so he's holding his judgement. He should be making a visit next month, but first my dad will be taking him to Athens to rest there for a little while before it gets too hot.'

'Oh, that should be nice for both of them.'

'As long as he's not there long enough to start any lengthy discussions,' Panos revealed. 'They disagree about practically everything, so if the conversation goes past small talk, they're going to be shouting at each other in no time.'

'Families, eh?' she nodded, knowing only too well what a difference of opinion could mean.

'Three generations of the same family and not one of us has anything in common with the others,' he shrugged. 'Luckily, we're happy to stay out of each other's way most of the time and let everyone just do what they want to do.'

'But you and your grandfather both have a creative flair; you have your art and he has the flowers, so both of those require a resourceful imagination.'

'Maybe, but I can't seem to imagine how I can fill the gaps in this display. It's missing something; just a small thing, but something that would pull it all together and enhance its celebration of nature.'

'I don't see it,' she said, as she gazed over every inch. 'Where do you think something's missing?'

'Here,' he pointed to a minute area at the front, before moving to an equally tiny space on the right, 'and here.'

'Well, there's nothing… Oh! That's weird. I didn't see anything wrong, but now you've pointed it out I can see that by placing some little things there it would keep the eyes following the loop, without causing a kind of hiccup in the middle. How clever you are!' she gushed.

'It's my artistic eye and yes, it does like to flow over a subject without being interrupted, but not everyone notices things like that. You obviously have an artistic talent too.'

'I don't know about that, but I am drawn to natural objects. I can somehow feel what they need and how they should be handled. I particularly like... wait! Of course,' she said as she hurried away, leaving Panos wondering if he had missed part of the conversation and unsure if he should follow.

He gazed after her and was unexpectedly struck by her fluid movements; it seemed as though she was floating on air and he admired the way her body extended like a ballerina as she reached across her stall to retrieve some hidden surprise. It was a simple action, but it almost took his breath away.

'I know what you need,' she said as she returned, beaming her delight at the possibility of having solved the problem.

'You do?' Panos croaked, his throat dry at the prospect of having his sudden desire discovered.

'My secret weapon,' she nodded. 'Hold out your hand.'

'My hand? Erm, OK,' he shivered. She couldn't possibly have known that he had just imagined sweeping his hand down the length of her elegant body, but he wasn't sure he was ready for it to happen in real life if she had. At this point, just taking his hand in hers would be a stunning attack on his senses.

'I believe this will make everything perfect,' she said as she placed her hand underneath his.

He took a deep breath as his nerves responded to her touch and then exhaled in shock as something cold and damp landed in his palm.

'What on earth?' he gulped as he tore his eyes away from hers and looked down at what she had just deposited among the fingers he had imagined might soon stroke her skin.

'Olives!' she announced, as though that one word explained everything.

'Olives?' he repeated, with the confusion in his mind appearing very clearly on his face.

'Yes, look!' she instructed as she took the olives back again and displayed a small number in each of the specific spaces Panos had previously identified. 'What do you think?'

'I think you're perfect,' he smiled. 'It's perfect, I mean.'

'I thought so,' she carried on. 'It just came to me suddenly.'

Panos understood the shock of a sudden realisation.

'It works really well,' he agreed, turning his attention to the display. 'Just filling the space without being obviously there.'

'Problem solved,' she nodded.

'Thank you, very much,' he said, thinking that it was possible his problems had only just begun. She was his work colleague and she had a fiancé. The kind of thoughts he was having were not acceptable and he had to brush them off. No doubt she had some faults he could concentrate on which would disperse this sudden infatuation? He would find them and make sure he didn't get carried away with his fantasies. It couldn't be that difficult, surely?

'You're welcome. Can I tell you a secret?'

'OK.' Let it be that she never cleans behind her ears, he hoped.

'I'm actually obsessed with olives. I help out every year with the olive picking and I would love, one day, to be able to produce and sell my own olive oil.'

'That doesn't sound like a secret; it sounds like a goal.'

'Well, it can never happen. My parents expect me to work on this stall for the rest of my life and I wouldn't be able to say I wanted to do anything else.'

'Whyever not? You should be able to do whatever you want.'

'Ha, if only you knew,' she said, her expression momentarily changing from a hopeful smile to a frustrated frown.

'So tell me,' he suggested.

'Let's just say they seem to be making all the decisions at the moment and my wants and needs, and especially my ambitions, are not something they're prepared to acknowledge. Anyway,' she continued, her face switching back to an expression of contented acceptance, 'more customers to attend to.'

He watched her break into a gorgeous welcoming smile to greet her new customers and wondered how she managed to pretend she was so happy, when only a moment ago her guard had slipped to reveal a deep injustice. He hoped she would find a way to fulfil her dream and decided that, while he was impatient to get back to his own career objectives, spending the summer in such inspirational company definitely would help to pass the time more quickly.

JUNE

The market place was more busy than usual that morning, probably due to the fact that the air conditioning was a welcome relief for many of the tourists who wanted to escape the unrelenting sunshine as they wandered around the town during what had been reported as a three-day mini-heatwave.

People appeared to be taking more time over their enquiries regarding the freshness of the fruit and vegetables and were engaging in deeper conversation about where on the island each of the products had been harvested, but the discussions did not appear to be resulting in extra sales in comparison to average days.

Some of the stall holders became a little frustrated and were trying to tempt their customers towards a purchase by offering discounts or free samples, but most of them were enjoying the chance to meet lots of holidaymakers who wanted to know more about the island and the wonderful items it could produce. They knew that a tourist's visit to the local market on a foreign holiday was always a moment to remember and they were happy to give their customers a flavour of the island, the gifts it had to offer, and a friendly conversation so that the whole event would stay in their minds once they returned home.

The corner unit was doing a good trade in frappe, or what the tourists called iced coffee, and the musky scent was drifting over towards the entrance, almost as though it was attempting to entice more passers-by into the vibrant atmosphere with its comforting familiarity. Any interested targets were then swept along by the earthy undertones of the calming vegetables, with their promise of healthy living and a virtuous lifestyle, before being suddenly bombarded by the colour and nose-wrinkling zesty delight of Kyriakos' expertly displayed fruit.

The combined temptation of invigorating aromas and vivid hues always ensured that the fruit stall had plenty of enthusiastic customers, but the added surprise of its charming owner's entertaining descriptions of the diverse harvesting processes, guaranteed that there was never a single item left over at the end of the day. Kyriakos had always been devoted to his business but his interactions with the public had recently risen to another level, appearing to have much more confidence and belief in himself now that he had stopped hiding the part of his character which he had been too scared to explore. His family had finally accepted that he was following a different path, but it was early days and he was enjoying the gradual journey of self-discovery and was excited for what it might lead to.

When customers could bear to tear themselves away from the citrussy intoxication, they found themselves in the soothing embrace of familiar flowers and soul-satisfying garden plants. The plants sold well to the residents and local businesses, but the visiting customers still felt the spirit-lifting benefits of touching the leaves and appreciating a living organism which could display such beauty and calmness. They would feel inspired by the natural miracle of creation and take some of the cut flowers away with them in order to continue that sensation.

By the time they reached Selina's stall with uplifting spices and nutritional honey, it would be exactly what they required to give them the drive to continue on with their shopping spree without running out of energy or motivation. At this stage, they would have only been halfway around the market and maybe needing a caffeine boost to be prepared for what the other stalls had to offer.

It was therefore very possible that many of the customers in the market place that morning had followed this route and were just debating whether to buy a coffee or soda when the fire alarm sounded and, after just a moment's confusion, all the stall holders started to instruct everyone to leave via the main entrance into the square.

'Just leave any baskets on the floor. It's probably just a false alarm and you will be able to come back and carry on in no time,' they were assured.

There was no obvious sign of flames or smoke so a few people took some persuading, but after several minutes everyone was out in the square and the firemen arrived to investigate the situation.

Most of the customers remained in the immediate area but some had wandered off, probably because they didn't have a basket of goods to return for, or they were too hot to stand under the full glare of the midday sun. While some of the crowd disappeared into the nearby cafés and restaurants, some of the café's customers exchanged places with them to see what all the fuss was about. Even more people appeared when a second fire truck arrived and an additional unit of firemen were available to appreciate.

No one seemed to be worried about why the alarm had sounded and were much more interested in the way the firemen jumped up onto the ladder and raised it above the roof to inspect the area for any signs of damage.

Shortly afterwards a local television crew arrived and began taking photographs and interviewing people in the crowd about what was happening, concentrating on those who had been inside when the incident was first acknowledged.

Word about the event seemed to have spread and some of the shop owners on the other side of the square had come to investigate. One or two from the Old Town had also made their way to the market to find out exactly what was happening.

Everyone seemed to be encouraged by the lack of smoke and took time to greet their fellow workers and find out how things were going for them. They complained about the temporary heatwave and the usual shenanigans of the local council, but they also expressed their pleasure about how the promenade area around the harbour had been renovated and was bringing more visitors to the area. It had taken a while to ensure that the harbourside and the castle were repaired after the earthquake a few years earlier, but everyone had come together to make sure it was done, offering support and assistance to any business owner who had been inadvertently affected.

That camaraderie and goodwill had increased over time, so when a possible fire had been reported at the market, it was no surprise that many of the local workers were quickly on hand to offer any help necessary. On this occasion, it seemed that everything was under control and so it simply turned into an unexpected break, where their friendships and acquaintances could be acknowledged and strengthened in a shared experience.

After some time, most of the crowd filtered away and the market stall holders were taking refuge under the shade of the bougainvillea at the entrance to the agora on the far side of the square. The caretaker and the manager were on hand to deal with the enquiries from the emergency services and it seemed that no cause had been found for the sounding of the alarm.

It had been traced to the device in the kitchen, which had been examined without finding any specific fault. There had been a slight delay in the remedy to the problem, as it required a complete replacement before the general public could be allowed to return, but the alarm kits which were kept on the vehicles were a new version which didn't fit with the facilities already in use in the market. Someone had been alerted at the fire station headquarters and they were on their way with one of the older types which would then take only ten minutes or so to replace.

The head fireman could only presume it was due to a build-up of humidity in the kitchen which could sometimes trigger an older device, or possibly something in the room was reflecting the strong sunshine which was beaming straight into the wash area. He advised getting blinds installed to shield the rays and to either have a small window open for ventilation or to re-direct the air conditioning to flow into the kitchen itself. The manager wasn't too impressed and appeared to dismiss the options, presumably due to the cost involved, but when it was pointed out that these recommendations would be going into the official report, meaning that the insurance could be invalid without acquiescing, he tersely nodded his agreement.

The staff were overjoyed to hear that they would no longer have to suffer in silence while they used the overheated kitchen, which was often nicknamed the sauna, but guessed the option of a small window would be the more likely resolution, rather than the luxury of enjoying the cooling waves of the air conditioner.

As the firemen posed for a few photographs before they left, the staff all made their way back inside the market place and began to tidy some of the items which had been dislodged in the rush to evacuate and during the firemen's investigations.

The baskets of abandoned goods waited like lost puppies looking for a home, but it seemed no one was about to return and claim them. By the time the general area had been tidied and the floor had been cleaned again, the main doors were opened to welcome back the happy throng who had been so enthralled by its contents only an hour earlier.

The silence was deafening.

The stall holders simply shrugged and began to empty the baskets and redistribute the goods to the correct areas so that they could be found easily, should the crowds finally return.

Of course, it was lunch time and that would be followed by siesta, so no one was expecting a repeat of the morning's excesses, but they knew the late afternoon customers would be back as usual after their day on the beach, or before their evening meal and that would mean a renewed sense of excitement within the market place, which was always something to look forward to.

And there was always tomorrow…

Selina saw Leandra hover around the flower stall as she approached, but Panos was deep in conversation with Kyriakos and neither of the boys noticed the way she expected to be automatically included.

'What's going on there then?' she asked with raised eyebrows as she finally moved on and joined her sister.

'Where?' Selina asked, as though she hadn't noticed the lack of attention which was usually very easy to achieve.

'With Panos and Kyriakos. They seem to be getting on very well, don't they?'

'Of course. They make a good team.'

'Oh, so they *are* together then? I did wonder, but now I can see how they are laughing together and teasing each other, it's obvious,' Leandra said with clear relief. She wasn't used to being ignored but if they only had eyes for each other that would explain why.

'What? No, I didn't mean that kind of team. I meant they work well together,' Selina corrected her. She didn't want any gossip flying around about her friends, especially if it was reported that it had started with her innocent comment.

'But you can see it for yourself, can't you? They're always hanging around together, although I thought Kyriakos was keen on Vitaly, but I could be wrong.'

'No, no, that can't be right. They just get on well together and neither of them have mentioned being gay, so I don't think you're on the right track there. It's not like they have to keep it a secret these days; everyone is happy to show if they are LGBTQ or non-binary because they have the freedom to be whoever they want to be.'

'You're kidding, right? I mean, I agree with your statement, but do you really think anyone outside our generation has really accepted it yet? Can you imagine mum's face if you said you were really a man and you wanted surgery to become the person you were supposed to be?' She laughed but they both knew it wasn't an amusing thought.

'No, but she would probably understand eventually,' Selina said unconvincingly.

'I just think that, as much as I'm sure Kyriakos is gay and seems to be confident in himself with that knowledge, he hasn't come out openly because either he can't face telling his parents, or when he told them, they went ballistic and told him to keep it a secret from their friends and neighbours. This is a small town and maybe it's just better for him if he doesn't broadcast the fact, but anyone can see how his behaviour tells the real story.'

'Oh, I never really thought about it, but I guess I can see what you mean,' Selina agreed. 'Should we tell him we know so that he could be more open around us?'

'No way. If he's comfortable, he'll share it with you. Otherwise, just leave him to his own devices.'

'Yes, you're probably right.'

'I am a bit unsure about this thing,' Leandra said as she swirled her hand between the two boys' stalls, 'with Panos, though. I was sure I'd seen some connection with him and Vitaly, but maybe I got that wrong. Unless he's already spoken for and now

Kyriakos has given up on him and started looking for another possibility.'

'I can't see that. Nothing about Panos makes me think he's gay,' Selina shrugged. 'But what do I know? I hadn't even realised what was going on under my nose until you just pointed it out, so maybe there is something,' she said quite despondently.

'Can you try to find out?' Leandra asked eagerly. 'Maybe you could chat to Panos and ask if he's seeing anyone? It will sound fine coming from you, now that you're officially engaged; he won't think you're hitting on him and he might be more open about his lifestyle.'

'Well, shouldn't we just let them get on with it? If nothing happens, we'll know he's not looking for that.' Selina wasn't keen on quizzing her new friend about such personal matters as she really didn't think it was any of her business.

'But if he's straight *and* single, I don't want to miss my opportunity,' Leandra gushed. 'He's been here just long enough to settle in now, so if he is looking for some romance it might be the time to let him know I'm interested. I mean, half the town is interested, look at him for God's sake; he's gorgeous.'

'I know,' Selina replied, having heard her sister use that phrase many times, more often than not about Panos.

'Oh! So even you're tempted then?' Leandra laughed. 'I honestly thought you'd been with Theo too long to remember how it felt to actually fancy someone.'

'No, I mean, I know you think he's gorgeous. You talk about nothing else,' Selina pouted. 'And, for your information, I can still appreciate a good-looking man without going overboard about it.'

'You could have fooled me. I've never seen you showing any interest in anyone, however innocently, and that includes your soon-to-be husband,' she huffed. 'I suppose Theo's attractive enough, especially when he's suited and booted, but you never gush about how gorgeous he is or how sexy he looks. Do you even notice anymore?'

'Of course I do!' she snapped back, though more out of annoyance than confirmation. 'Not everyone wears their heart on their sleeve, you know.'

'Maybe you should try it now and again. I'm sure Theo doesn't hear it often enough, and men like to know these things so they don't feel like they're being taken for granted.'

'I don't take him for granted. He knows exactly how I feel about him and we often tell each other how happy we are to be together. Just because I don't broadcast it to everyone I see, doesn't mean it isn't important.'

'I'm sure you do care for each other deeply and I do know how close you are, but there doesn't seem to be much excitement, or flirtation or, I don't know, hot damn sexiness!' she growled. 'Whenever people see you together, they think "Aw" instead of "Grr" and that just makes you look like sister and brother.'

'We don't need excitement or flirtation and our sex life is just fine, thank you. We don't need to try and make it into something when we've already found what we want and, rather than sister and brother, I like to think we're soulmates. We're in step with each other and don't need to keep trying to create any kind of spark when we've already got a cosy fire to snuggle up to.'

'And there it is,' Leandra exhaled heavily. 'When you're using words like cosy and snuggle it's clear that you are acting more like friends. Maybe very, very good friends, but friends all the same. If I was talking about the man of my dreams, I would be using the idea of a roaring fire, so boiling hot that I would have to tear off all my clothes and grind against his body until I was a wet breathless mess. I certainly wouldn't be snuggling.'

'That's because you've never had true love,' Selina replied, hiding her anger behind a condescending comment.

'But I have; many, many times. It might have only lasted a week, or a night, or an hour, but I've felt how amazing it can be to be with the one person who means everything to you in that one defining moment and that's as true a feeling of love as I can imagine. As time passes you lose that spark and, along with it, the energy and desire that keeps the flame alive. I've been lucky to be able to move on without fear when it's no longer exciting, but I think some people aren't quite as brave and they hold onto something half-decent for security and familiarity and then it just becomes a habit.'

'You're saying that I stayed with Theo out of habit?' Selina asked through clenched teeth, with a harsh tone and fiery eyes, while just about managing to keep her voice at a respectable level.

'Not intentionally, but probably, yes. Look, I know you've been happy with him all this time and that's great, but all this wedding talk has got me wondering if,' she took a breath. 'Well, if you're doing the right thing.'

'We're not getting married tomorrow; it's not like we're rushing into anything. We'll get married when we're ready and the family know that.' She managed to say the words without revealing the stress she was already feeling about the new wedding date, which was now being regularly debated at family gatherings.

'But that's the whole point. Can I be honest with you?' she asked, before immediately continuing. 'I can't help thinking that if I was madly in love with someone, enough to want to spend the rest of my life with them, I would want it to happen straightaway. Obviously,' she smiled, 'there would have to be enough time to organise the wedding of the century, but as soon as it was humanly possible to arrange, I would want to be Mrs Whatever and spend every minute of the day together. And this is the thing; I'm having trouble understanding how, if you love each other so much, you don't just want to get on with it.' Leandra ended her statement gently and seemed genuinely to want to understand where Selina was coming from.

'There's no great secret; we've said it a thousand times. We're just really happy with how we are right now and don't want anything to change that,' Selina replied simply and with some weariness at the constant repetition of her wishes.

'But you can't stay like this forever. What about a home of your own? Waking up together every morning? Making some mini Selinas and mini Theos, or even one of each if you end up with more twins? You can't stay twenty-seven forever, locked in some kind of time capsule.'

'You seem to be managing that easily enough!' Selina snapped back, finally having heard enough about how her life couldn't continue in the happy way she hoped.

'But I'm still single. We singletons seem to stay younger for longer and so we can avoid the kind of responsibility that relationships bring, until we're ready to change. When you're in a relationship you're already on the road to change and development and it's not possible to stay where you are and just look after yourself. That would just be selfish and very inconsiderate. You've only been able to use this argument because Theo's saying the same thing.'

'That's because we do actually both want the same thing; we're on the same page.'

'You're both selfish. Either that, or you're both too scared to be honest about how you really feel and it's easier just to stay how you are now rather than face your fears and admit that you don't want to move forward together.'

'That's enough,' Selina said coarsely.

'I'm sorry, but it had to be said. I've been trying to have this conversation with you for weeks and, to be honest, I was waiting for a quieter moment, but it just happened now and I'm glad it did. You need to think about what you really want and whether or not

Theo is an important part of it. Don't just go along with all these wedding plans because you've been backed into a corner. Stand up for yourself and admit what you really need in your life. If it is Theo, I will support you one hundred percent, but please, take some time to think it through before you make the worst mistake of your life, just because you were too scared to say how you really feel.'

Selina stared hard while her nostrils flared with every angry breath she took, but she didn't dare to form any words in response and Leandra simply shrugged and left.

Luckily, it was a quiet part of the day and Selina had time to recover herself after Leandra's outburst. She looked over to where Panos and Kyriakos had calmed down from their earlier exploits and appeared to be listening to something on their phones. There was a look of utter devotion on Kyriakos' face, but Panos had an expression of slight confusion and she wondered if their stance had anything to do with the romantic overtones her sister had mentioned.

She hoped that, if they were to begin a relationship, they would both be happy because she was quite fond of each of them but somehow, she just couldn't imagine them together. Kyriakos loved the nightlife and was always the centre of attention, but Panos was very quiet and reserved and seemed to prefer to avoid the brashness of evening entertainment in the centre of town. The thought sent a shiver down her spine because Theo and herself behaved in exactly the same manner; he loved the nightlife and she avoided it. She wasn't sure what that meant in the grand scheme of things, but she couldn't stop an image from replaying in her head of Kyriakos and Theo on their night out, which somehow stimulated the vision of Panos inviting her to sit next to him on a bench overlooking the calm and peaceful sea.

She was confused and excited at the same time, but quickly brushed the thought away as having been aroused by what Leandra had said. She didn't want to start second guessing herself or her relationship so she gave herself a little shake and decided to wipe that conversation from her mind by closing her eyes for a moment. When she opened them again, it would be forgotten and she would continue as before.

She was not expecting the first thing that she would see to be Panos standing in front of her, gazing with curiosity as he tried to work out what she was doing.

'Is that some kind of meditation? Because if it is, I would say this isn't the ideal place,' he smiled.

'Oh, no, it was… Erm, I was just taking a rest.'

'If you're tired, I can cover your stall,' he offered pleasantly. 'It's no trouble.'

'That's very kind, but I'm fine. I just needed a moment.' She would have loved to unload about her annoying sister's accusations, but he wasn't the one to talk to. She couldn't actually think of anyone she could talk to because she would naturally go to Theo with any of her problems, but not this. Definitely not this.

'Well, just let me know if you need anything,' he shrugged. 'Everyone has been so kind to welcome me here, I'm happy to pay it back anytime.'

'We're just like one big happy family,' she smiled, cheering herself at the thought. 'Looks like you've made a good friend in Kyriakos…'

She wasn't sure why she'd brought up the subject; she definitely wasn't trying to find out any gossip for her insatiable sister, but she had a sudden urge to know more about him.

'Oh, he is *so* funny,' Panos nodded. 'He makes me laugh a lot and seems to keep everyone amused with his ideas and opinions.'

'He does seem different this year; somehow he's more open and talkative. We would often have discussions about things that were happening around the town, but now he seems to want to create new things to enjoy and he's always arranging nights out which he never did before.'

'He did say he feels lighter now that his parents know the truth. It must have been very restrictive to his personality to have to hide that side of himself from everyone.'

'Because… he's gay?' she asked quietly.

'Yeah. Obviously, he doesn't broadcast the fact because his family are still getting used to it, but he told me how he met a special person last year and she helped him to face his fears and express what he really wanted out of life. Now he can be true to who he really is and enjoy whatever life brings his way.'

'That's good,' she nodded, trying to ignore the way his comments echoed those of Leandra only a short time earlier.

'It's wonderful. It means a new start and a lot more happiness, which we all need.'

'So… is that a new start for you, too? Are you finding happiness together?'

'Well, obviously I'm having a new start this year, by making new friends and discovering a different way of living for a while; I suppose it's because of these things that I'm feeling happier.'

'You seemed to be having fun there together,' she continued, trying to show support for what she envisioned as a burgeoning romance. 'It looked as though he had you thinking things over.'

'He's an absolute nutcase!' he laughed. 'He was trying to convince me that Taylor Swift sings his name in one of her songs.'

'Huh?' Selina was totally thrown off course with that comment.

'He kept singing the line with part of it as his name, but I said he was crazy, so he got the song up on Spotify and made me listen through the whole thing.'

'But it's not his name?' She meant the observation as a question, but it sounded more like a statement because, clearly, Taylor Swift would not sing about Kyriakos. Surely?

'Of course not. It's not even a real line in the song, it's more like backing vocals, but definitely not his name. Someone's kind of doing a chant in the background and there's no way of understanding what's being said, but it sounded like "key in a hole" to me.'

'And he thinks it sounds like Kyriako?'

'Of course, and it's only once in the whole of the song, really faint and in the background. No one else would ever have heard that so I'm pretty sure he's been listening to all kinds of music and just looking for anything that sounds even vaguely like his name. He's hilarious!'

'I'm glad you've met someone who makes you laugh,' she said, unthinkingly placing her hand on his arm. 'It's wonderful that you've found each other and I hope that means you'll stay around for a bit longer than you planned.'

His hand automatically covered hers as he reacted to the sensation, while her words slowly unfolded themselves in his mind to gradually reveal what she was trying to express.

'Oh, no! We're not a couple,' he said, as his hand squeezed hers to silently indicate how wrong she was about where his affections lay.

'But you're getting on so well; you look really good together.' She wasn't sure why she said that as she still didn't think they did, but maybe he just needed a little encouragement to take things to the next level.

'That's interesting because, even though he makes me laugh, we couldn't be more different.'

'But Theo and I are quite different and we're still happy together.'

'Yes,' he said, as he quickly removed his hand from hers. It left a cold vacuum. 'But you like men and he likes women, so it works for you. Kyriakos likes men and I like women, so that doesn't work for us.'

'Oh! I'm so sorry. I didn't know…'

'It's fine. We haven't discussed my romantic life, so you would have no way of knowing. Not that I have a romantic life at the moment,' he finished abruptly.

'Well, I'm sure it's not for lack of opportunity,' she said, much too quickly. 'I mean, there's a lot of lovely single ladies out there you could have fun getting to know.' Leandra would be glad to hear that he was available, if she bothered to tell her.

'I'm sure, but I have other things on my mind right now.'

'You mean, your business?'

'Yes. It's at a bit of a standstill while I'm here, but I've had an enquiry to capture an image of the flamingos at the salt-lake so I need to see if I can fit that in around the market work.' It wasn't the only thing that was increasingly occupying his mind, but he couldn't tell her that.

'What a wonderful opportunity. You must find a way to make it work; it would make the perfect painting. I really love being around there, it's so peaceful and free and the air seems to be so fresh it clears away any bad thoughts or feelings.'

'That sounds like you're involved in something physical. Is it swimming? Running? Cycling?'

'Horse-riding. I don't have my own horse, but there are stables nearby where they do excursions for visitors along the beach. I help out there sometimes so they've come to trust me and they're happy to let me exercise one of the horses now and then if they've been quiet. It's absolutely the best feeling.'

'It's not something I've ever done, but it sounds amazing.'

'You should give it a try. I can take you sometime, if you like.'

'Maybe. I'll bear it in mind.' He wasn't sure about riding one of the animals, but he knew he would love to see her on horseback, wild and untamed and loving life. He would love to paint that.

'You might meet someone there who you could spend more time with,' she suggested, trying to be supportive of his possible desire to find romance.

'I'm not really looking for a new relationship just now,' he told her. It was only a half lie. 'I've just come out of a serious relationship which had run its course and I'm having a bit of time for myself just now.'

'I'm sorry. I didn't mean to push you, I just thought you might need someone to introduce you to new people, but I'm sure you'll have no trouble making friends when you're ready.'

'Thank you. I'm quite happy with the friends I've made already, so that's more than enough for now,' he smiled warmly. Yes, the friends he was now lucky to know were exactly what he needed at the moment and he was ready to enjoy their company; he just wasn't sure how he would be able to leave some of them at the end of the summer.

'Looks like someone needs attention,' she nodded towards the flower stall as an elderly couple approached.

'That's what I'm here for,' he joked as he made his way back to the stall. He was happy to give the couple some attention as they chose a suitable posy, but he would much rather have given even more attention to the young woman he was growing closer to, who would haunt his dreams that night in a Lady Godiva vision of equine power and beauty.

Theo and Selina were sitting with Rosie on their regular afternoon break, enjoying the respective delights of ice cream, frappe and iced tea.

The couple were explaining to their weekly visitor what was happening with the flower stall and how Old Mr Mylonas had just called to say hello to everyone on his return from Athens. His wife had decided they should take an extended break to escape the heat of the high season, so that they could relax and be more comfortable with her sister who had married a German man and was living in Hamburg. He wasn't too keen to be leaving the island, but he acknowledged that his stall was in good hands and he was quite interested to see the different flora of another country, as he had never joined his wife on her previous summer visits and there hadn't been much to see on their occasional festive holidays there.

Theo was surprised that he seemed to have recovered very quickly, but Selina reminded him that it was a mild stroke and had been caught quickly, so he probably wouldn't have any lasting issues from it, but everyone (including the old man himself) knew that his working days were over and the stall would be transferred to new owners next year.

'Unless Panos decides to take over, after all,' Theo suggested. 'He said he was enjoying himself on the island when we were talking yesterday, so I suppose he might be too settled to leave before much longer.'

'Not when most of his business dealings are in the north,' Selina said firmly. She knew it was a temporary situation.

'But that's just his office,' Theo said dismissively. 'If he's an artist he can draw, or paint, anywhere and it would be easy enough to set up an office facility in a spare room wherever he was.'

'That's where he has all his contacts and he stores his work there too. It sounds like the best place for his exhibitions and he's on his way to creating a name for himself, so he'd be crazy to just leave it in the hope of setting up somewhere else.' Selina was happy to support Panos' decision, but she wasn't quite as happy about it as she sounded; she would definitely miss him when he left.

'What kind of work does he do?' Rosie asked. 'Portraits?'

'I've no idea, he doesn't really talk about it,' Theo said.

'Oh, I, erm... I think he has done some portraits but I heard him saying he likes to do landscapes and scenes of nature, with flowers or animals.'

'Who did he say that to?' Theo asked with a frown. 'Must have been Kyriakos; those two have been inseparable for weeks.'

'Probably,' Selina nodded. She hadn't told Theo about her regular chats with Panos because it had only started as a casual chat between neighbours and they were both on the other side of the room. As they'd got to know each other, he had revealed more about himself and they had shared a few moments which had felt really special, so she didn't want to spread information about his private life as though it was general gossip. She knew that if Panos had stayed around, they would have become very firm friends, but as he would eventually be leaving, she didn't want to invest in such a close connection only to have to learn to live without it afterwards.

'Unless it was Leandra. She seems to be popping in all the time now and it's always the flower stall she heads for first.'

'Yes,' Selina sighed. 'I've told her not to make it so obvious, but she's determined to get friendly with him.'

'Sounds like she wants more than friendship and, knowing Leandra, she usually gets what she wants,' Theo scoffed.

'I think she scares him,' Selina shrugged. 'One time he thought she was me and offered a sample of honey he'd bought from a local farmer. She couldn't get in there quickly enough and then he realised who she was when she started to bestow her knowledge of one hundred and one uses for honey.'

'I'm guessing they weren't all specifically involved with food preparation,' Rosie giggled.

'Not even remotely. He was so grateful when I rescued him.'

'How on earth did he mix you up?' Theo asked, dumbfounded. 'You're *nothing* alike.'

'Erm, they're identical twins?' Rosie scowled in confusion.

'Only to a stranger. They look and dress completely differently and as soon as one of them opens their mouth you know who is who.'

'I'm not sure if you mean that as an insult or a compliment,' Selina pondered.

'Neither. It's just a fact. She's all make-up and hairspray and you're natural and casual.'

'Still not sure either of us come out of that description well.'

'I'm just pointing out your differences. Hey, isn't that your cousin?' Theo asked, quickly taking the opportunity to change the subject from one which had no satisfactory outcome.

'Yes, it is. Hi!' she shouted over and waved as the lady with a bag of melons caught her eye.

The next moment seemed to happen in slow motion as Selina's cousin raised her hand to wave, allowing the bag to swing and drop one of its contents onto the pathway. It rolled forward and she rushed to grab it before it succumbed to the gravity of the small hill, crashing into the bicycle of the Dutch tourist who had veered off his course to take in the beauty of the square.

Everyone ended up on the floor and the fruit was spread in all directions.

Selina and Theo jumped up and raced over immediately. Rosie stood, but wasn't sure she was needed and if they all left, their refreshments would be removed, so she stayed put.

Luckily there was no damage to the bicycle and only a few grazes on the cousin's arm and the Dutch man's very long legs. People started to gather with the melons they had rescued and it seemed the skins had taken a minimal impact, so they would be fine to use as the freebie treats for which they were intended.

Selina decided to walk her cousin back to work and clean up her superficial wounds, but Theo returned to the table where his ice cream was rapidly melting as there was no need for any extra assistance.

'That was a bit scary. Lucky you were around to help out,' Rosie stated admiringly.

'I'm glad we were there for her, but anyone else would have rushed to her aid if we'd been at work,' Theo assured her. 'Everywhere you go on this island, someone knows someone, and if they don't know you, they at least know who you are, or who you're related to.'

'That's so nice,' Rosie said, with a warm glow from the idea of true camaraderie.

'It can be,' he admitted, 'but it can also be a pain in the neck if you're trying to keep a low profile.'

'I suppose so, but I'd be so happy if I thought someone would have my back like that.'

'Surely your friends would take care of you, if you needed them?'

'I'm sure they would, if I had any,' she gulped, the truth forcing its way out in a plea for understanding.

'Ah, of course, you moved from Kefalos…'

'And that would have been fine if I had friends of my own, because I would still be able to meet up with them. I wish I'd made some friends outside of my relationship, but until it was over, I didn't realise how much I would need them.'

'Have they all sided with him then? Aren't any of the other girlfriends or wives prepared to support you?'

'I was never very close to any of them, to be honest. We only got together as a group; either all the men did something together or the couples did, but never the women on their own. Unless they did, but never invited me, which is a possibility.'

'They were all Greek?'

'Yes, but I don't think they were prejudiced. Maybe they just knew I wouldn't last, in the end.'

'Well then, it's good that you're now friends with everyone at the market,' he said in an effort to cheer her up.

'I don't know if we're friends,' she smiled shyly. 'They probably just like me because I bring a coachload of people to shop there every week.'

'Of course they do!' he laughed. 'But that's the best way to show your support of them and their businesses, so it's a great base to forming friendships in the future.'

'I hope so; they're a great bunch,' she said genuinely.

'Well then, I hope you'll come and spend some time with us all next month on my name day. It's going to be on Sunday this year, so we're all going to the beach for an afternoon barbeque. Goodness knows who'll get burned first and whether it will be from the sun or the flames of the grill!' he grinned.

'Really? Oh, that sounds wonderful. I only work on occasional Sundays, so I can arrange it to be my day off, if you're sure?'

'What? Sure it's going to be my name day? Sure we're going to have a barbeque? Sure that someone will end up getting burned? Yes, yes and yes! Book a day off and I'll come to pick you up beforehand.

You might have to get a taxi back though, if the usual alcohol consumption is anything to go by.'

'No problem. Thank you so much, I'm looking forward to it already.'

She appreciated the fact that he glossed over her insecurities about being invited to the group celebration which wouldn't normally include an outsider. She knew most of the staff by name and certainly wouldn't feel out of place on the day, even though she might very well be the only non-Greek there. They were all such a friendly bunch that she knew it was going to be a fun afternoon and it would give her a good chance to speak to all of them on a more personal basis.

She hoped that she would be able to relax with a great group of people and maybe dismiss the constant voice in her head saying that she should just give up, accept defeat and go home. It might be difficult to make a new start as a single person, but it wasn't impossible and if she could stop allowing random thoughts of Theo to invade her mind, she might even find another singleton she could enjoy spending time with. Panos was a nice guy, but even though she hadn't felt any chemistry with him, it was possible they might have something in common and he might be able to distract her from the growing torment of wanting someone she could never have.

She knew that he was probably leaving after the main summer season and that there was a high possibility of her needing to do the same thing, but in the meantime, she might be able to enjoy the next few months in pleasant company and, at the very least, make a few good friends.

She was willing to give it a try, because she wasn't quite ready to give up. Not yet.

JULY

Theo had been up for hours, checking all the details for his name day celebration and finalising the timings of deliveries so that everything would flow smoothly.

Kyriakos had pleaded to be involved in some way, but Theo wanted to be sure that everything went without a hitch, so he had organised everything to the finest detail before allowing his friend to oversee the arrangement so that he felt that he had played an important role. It meant that, although he knew what to expect, the final vision would be a surprise when he finally turned up to find everyone waiting for him.

That also gave him time to go and collect Rosie which would be a good opportunity to clear his head on the journey of around forty minutes in total. He probably shouldn't have had the extra drinks after his discussion with Selina the previous night, but he was wound up and needed something strong to make him forget their disagreement.

They never argued, but they did disagree over some things and he'd realised it was happening quite regularly recently. He'd become particularly annoyed over the arrangements for his name day barbeque when she kept reminding him that it was a "celebration" and not the "party" he kept referring to. He'd kept quiet for a while, but then felt that was what he was doing more and more just to keep the peace and he actually strongly disagreed with her stance. It might indeed be a celebration, but it was also a chance for him to get together with friends and family and that, to him, made it a party. He wanted it to be a party. He didn't want people to just sit around quietly on the beach and have a swim and a sleep, he wanted everyone to be dancing and playing games and having so much fun that they would be talking about it for months afterwards.

She said he couldn't force people to join in with the activities if they just wanted a quiet Sunday afternoon, and he agreed, but he said it was his name day and he should be able to have the kind of fun he preferred with whoever was willing to join in with him. There was a temporary silence and he wondered if she would suggest that he was being a little selfish, although that would probably steer them towards a more aggressive discussion which would be entirely out of character for them. She simply took a deep breath and said that he could entertain the ones who wanted to join in and she would chat with the ones who wanted a more relaxing time, which was what would have happened anyway.

They had parted on that note and wished each other a good night, but it had left Theo with an uneasy feeling and it had taken a few glasses of whisky to relax him enough to be able to sleep.

He set off for Kardamena and was half inclined to take the long way round over the mountain as the views were spectacular and he hardly ever got to see them these days, but he knew Rosie would be waiting and didn't want to worry her with a late arrival. The road was slightly busier than he had expected, but he knew lots of Greek families had Sunday as a day off and they often made the effort to spend their time out of the resort where they lived, to give them a change of scenery and a sense of escape, especially in the busy high season which was now under way.

He would have liked to have spent the day in another resort as a special treat, but he couldn't expect all his friends and workmates to make the journey too, so it would have to wait for another time and he would much rather have everyone around him today, even if it meant staying local.

Rosie was waiting as he pulled up and opened the door.

'Wow, you look gorgeous,' he said instinctively.

'Because I usually look so awful?' she grinned playfully.

'No, I didn't mean that…'

'I'm just teasing. Thank you, it's nice of you to say so,' she said as she got comfortable in her seat.

'You just look really different.'

'Again, thank you for pointing out how bad I usually look.'

'Not bad; you never look bad,' he said reassuringly. 'Just more... tidy.'

'OK, you'd better stop now,' she laughed.

'Yes, I'm making a mess of it. I've just never seen you look so...' he hesitated.

'Colourful?' she finished. She wished he had said "beautiful" but that was probably too much, and he had already started the conversation with "gorgeous" which was more than she could have hoped for. 'It's because the guiding uniform is so drab and I have to tie my hair back. Some people don't even recognise me when I wear my own clothes.'

'Well that's crazy. I would recognise your eyes anywhere; I've never seen anything quite as blue as that before,' he said, revealing more than he knew he was aware of.

'Except for the blue of that perfect sky today,' she replied quickly, her breath catching at the surprise of his comment.

'Isn't it?' he answered, slipping into gear and moving away. 'I'm glad we've got the air conditioning today or we'd be roasted by the time we get to the beach.'

'I saw some people making their way up the mountain this morning and they had a picnic to enjoy in the cooler temperatures up there. I was very jealous.'

'Oh, that would be a lovely way to spend the day,' he said, suddenly imagining the view from that perfect spot, with a tempting picnic and good company...

'You should take Selina up there one weekend; I'm sure you could do with the break now it's so busy in the high season.'

He had to contain his laugh. 'There's no way Selina would just sit there eating and drinking; she'd have to be horse riding or cycling or running.'

'Maybe you could do both?'

He let his laugh free this time. 'Not me! I'm not the active type. I'd rather enjoy the food and wine in pleasant surroundings, while Selina likes to feel at one with nature and become part of the scenery by getting into places off the beaten track.'

'She does like the nature aspect, I know,' Rosie nodded. 'She was telling me about how much she loves watching the changing flora and fauna over the seasons.'

'And they love her too. It's always *me* who gets stung by a bee, or ends up covered in mosquito bites, or stands on a scorpion, or falls into the nettles and thistles. It would be difficult to describe which is the most painful, but I don't put myself in that position anymore.'

'Oh dear,' she laughed. 'That sounds like me when I went on a camping trip. I was constantly getting stung or bitten and when we went foraging for food, I fell into a blackberry bush which had the biggest thorns you've ever seen!'

'You had to search for food?' he asked, with undisguised horror.

'Not for our main meals, but it was an attempt to show us how we could eat food that grows in the wild. I'm afraid it wasn't for me; give me a takeaway any day!'

'Now you're talking my language. I love my mum's home-cooked meals, or something traditional from a local taverna, but if it's up to me I'd rather have a pizza and a cold beer.'

'Who wouldn't?' she shrugged knowingly.

They happily chatted about their favourite types of takeaway throughout the journey to the beach, where they arrived to find everyone already enjoying a drink and some nibbles.

'Rosie! Come and sit with me while Theo sorts everything out,' Selina called, indicating a seat which she had reserved on a nearby table.

They got some drinks and a few peanuts to keep them going until the food was ready, which looked as though it would take a while to organise. They complimented each other on their clothes and Selina made the same observation that Rosie looked very different out of uniform. She loved the loose blonde curls which weren't usually in evidence, but suggested she might need to tie it up as usual with the dangerous combination of wind and sand already causing a little chaos around the barbeque.

'Yes, I've brought a couple of scrunchies. I knew we were on the beach but I thought we might be inside for the food first and I wanted to dress up for a change.'

'Well, you look beautiful,' Selina smiled.

'Thank you.' It was a lovely thing to say, but didn't seem to have the same effect as it would have done, had it have come from Theo's mouth.

'Oh, there goes the music,' Selina said, trying to disguise her annoyance.

'Ooh, I love this song,' Rosie replied, jiggling in her seat. 'After a couple of drinks, I won't be able to stay off the dance floor, if there can be such a thing on the beach!'

'You can bet Theo's worked out a space for dancing and some games he has planned. It looks like anyone who wants to play a bit of volleyball will have to miss out today,' Selina pouted.

'Ugh, I hate volleyball,' Rosie replied forcefully, failing to notice her friend's dismay. 'I mean, I don't mind watching the guys getting all hot and sweaty while I have a drink or something, but half an hour's enough, isn't it? Then it just gets boring, and I'd rather lie on a sunbed to top up my tan than run around getting sticky and breathless in this heat.'

'You could always cool off in the sea?' Selina suggested. 'That seems to be what most of the lads do after a game and everyone just piles in after them whether they're celebrating a win or not.' She remembered a few times she'd been part of the winning team and looked forward to the general celebration by being thrown high into the air and enjoying the sensation of crashing into the refreshing water as a welcome relief from the exertion.

'Hmm, I'm not much of a swimmer. I like a paddle and the occasional dip, but I don't like getting my hair wet and I'm not keen on the after effect of salty grains all over my body. Ugh.'

'Right,' Selina nodded. She had become quite friendly with Rosie, but she was beginning to realise that she really didn't know her at all.

'Although I'm happy to join in today because it looks like we're going to have some fun. It's nice to see so many of the other stall holders here and it's a treat to have more than an hour to chat with everyone.'

'Yes, you can take your time today, although I think Theo's going to be mingling with everyone else most of the time, so neither of us will probably have the chance to talk to him very much.'

'Oh, I didn't think of that,' Rosie frowned as she took a sip of her drink. 'I suppose it would have been more romantic for you both to spend some time on your own today.'

'Romance doesn't come into it today,' Selina replied, more forcefully than she had intended. 'It's his name day, rather than a birthday or anniversary, so it's something we share with everyone.'

'Still, it would be nice to celebrate something so special on your own. Maybe you'll be able to do something nice together tonight?' Rosie hoped it didn't sound as though she was fishing for information. That wasn't what she had intended, at least, she didn't think it was.

'After he's three sheets to the wind? Is that the right way to say it? Anyway, all he'll be fit for after today is an early night.'

Rosie bit back the temptation to say that she would love the chance to have an early night with someone as wonderful as Theo, even if he was pretty drunk. In fact, it might be even more fun if he was tipsy enough forget his responsibilities for a while and just make the most of the moment without any expectations – or was that just what she wanted for herself?

'Well, it does look as though he's enjoying himself,' she said, recovering her thoughts, 'and I suppose that's the main thing. There'll be other days you can enjoy some romance together.'

'Maybe years ago, but that changes when you've been with someone a long time,' Selina pointed out, quite openly. 'That kind of stuff isn't really important after a while.'

'Romance? Isn't that always important?' Rosie asked in amazement.

'I don't think so. When we first got together, we were young and trying to impress each other and then we moved on to expressing how much we felt for each other; there was certainly a lot of romance in those days,' Selina said with a suggestive grin. 'But we're more or less ten years down the line now and we've said everything we can think of, we've bought all the trinkets we need, we've given each other as many surprises as we can handle and we've expressed our love for each other in every way possible.'

'That sounds like you've just given up,' Rosie said in disbelief.

'It doesn't mean we love each other any less. In fact, it just reassures us that we have genuinely assured each other of our true devotion. We don't even need to say it anymore, or mark each anniversary with a huge gathering just to prove we're good together. It's like we're two sides of the same coin and we just fit together perfectly. We love and trust each other, so there's no need for all those romantic displays that couples want in the early days and we're happy enough together not to have to keep showing it to maintain what we've created.'

Selina stopped talking before it began to sound like she was proving a point. No one had really asked her that question before, so she was surprised by how she found herself explaining it and the way it might come across as some kind of hopeful justification rather than a valid reason for the redundancy of naïve romance in their relationship. She'd had a lot of time to think things over since her conversation with Leandra.

'I hear what you're saying,' Rosie began calmly. She heard it but she didn't understand it. She certainly didn't believe it. No one could live without romance; what would be the point? 'But don't you miss those early days, when he would surprise you with a bunch of flowers, or take you for a lovely meal on your birthday, or buy you a piece of jewellery, just because he wanted to see you smile?'

'They were good times,' Selina agreed. 'But I don't miss them. I had them all, so they stay with me as memories now. If we tried all that again it would just seem pointless, because we've already done it all, over and over. We enjoy a calmer version of romance now where we just know each other so well that we're comfortable to be together. Sometimes we can spend the whole evening together and not even speak! I think that's what people dream of and I definitely can't imagine my life without him.'

Rosie understood how Selina couldn't imagine her life without Theo. She knew she was becoming more attracted to him herself and wondered how she would cope without their weekly chats and his lovely smile. What she couldn't understand was how they could spend the whole evening together and not even speak; how was that supposed to be a good thing? The only way she could imagine being together with Theo for hours and not saying a word, would be if they were asleep or, preferably, too busy kissing every inch of each other's bodies to be able to string a sentence together.

'Sounds like you've met your soul mate,' she said. It was the only phrase she could think of which would sound like she was accepting what her friend was saying. It sounded as though Selina was in love and happy with how things were going in her relationship, but it sounded all wrong to Rosie. She would want romance all through her life, whoever she was with, and she wouldn't be able to live without it if she'd been lucky enough to be with Theo.

'He's my best friend,' Selina nodded. 'And it looks like he's ready with the food. Coming?'

'No, I'll wait for everyone to get a plateful first. I'm just going for a paddle and I'll get mine in a bit.'

Selina went to join the group who were deciding what kind of food they wanted and testing out how well, or otherwise, each of the items had been barbequed.

Rosie allowed the noise of the gathering to disappear from her mind as she found some peace in the cool shallow waves, lapping at the edge of the pebbly beach.

She was thinking over Selina's last comment about Theo being her best friend and she cringed at the idea, just as she had done whenever she'd heard it in the past. A lot of people said their partner was their best friend and, true, you would hope they possessed the same qualities, but she never truly accepted the description.

A best friend was someone you could tell your inner secrets to, someone who would support all your choices and would always help you out in a crisis. You would certainly expect to receive the same attention from your partner, but the physical closeness you would enjoy with them and the total submission you would experience under their touch was nothing like you would expect from any kind of friend. Even a best friend. There was a definite difference between a lover and a friend and Rosie would never believe anyone could be truly both.

She wondered if Theo felt the same as Selina, if he would describe his relationship in the same casual way, that they were best friends. If she had been lucky enough to be his partner, she would make sure he never saw her as any kind of friend by devoting all her energy into making him feel special, desirable and very, very wanted. From what Selina had just said, it sounded like they had fallen into some kind of routine where they just muddled along together and that seemed like such a waste, for both of them.

She wished that she could be with Theo to bring some romance and excitement into his life, but she accepted that he loved Selina and decided that, however hard it might be, she had a duty to find a way of introducing that spark back into their relationship. She really liked Selina and had such strong feelings for Theo that it was only right for her to try to create more fulfilment in his life by increasing the happiness between the two of them. She wanted him to have the best life possible and if that couldn't be with her, and she really knew that it couldn't, it would give her enormous pleasure to help him rediscover that feeling with the woman he obviously loved.

It wouldn't be easy for her, but she just wanted to know that he was happy and if she could create that feeling for him, it would go some way to making her loneliness slightly less painful.

After the food had been served, to rave reviews, most people were relaxing on their sunbeds, although there was a bit of exuberant dancing from some of the younger crowd.

Theo had organised a few games, but everyone needed a little time to recover from the opulent feast before the afternoon really got under way, so he was happy to chat when Panos approached to thank him for the wonderful food they had just enjoyed.

'It's my pleasure. I'm just glad that everyone has turned up to celebrate with me today.'

'You certainly know a lot of people.'

'That's what comes from living on such a small island, though at least half of them are distant relatives. It's strange how we only get together for family occasions, but with so many of us, we seem to be celebrating all the time,' Theo laughed.

'That must be nice,' Panos said with genuine warmth. 'I know most Greek families have lots of different levels of relations, but mine is fairly small and we seem to be scattered throughout the country so it's never a big gathering for us. Still nice to catch up with them though,' he added, so that his friend wouldn't think he was quite as lame as he sounded.

'Well, you are welcome to share mine anytime. There's a few of them who probably think you're one of us anyway and they'll be convinced you must be a distant cousin if you turn up at the next one of these things.'

'Once a year is probably enough, hey? Unless, I'm thinking maybe you're planning an engagement party... Didn't I hear somewhere that you've set a date for the wedding?'

'You've probably heard it everywhere, but that doesn't mean it's happening,' Theo said rather forcefully.

'Oh, I'm sorry. I'm not sure where I heard it, but it seemed like a done deal. Obviously someone was speaking out of turn.'

'No, they're probably not. My parents have let it be known that Selina and I will be getting married in three years, but that only happened because I said it wouldn't be before that. They kept hounding us for a date and when I thought I'd given them the perfect reason to back off, they just took it as a starting point.'

'Ah, that's parents for you. Mine are still having trouble believing that I have a successful career with something they perceive as a hobby. They're still waiting for me to announce that I'm moving to Athens with them to train as an accountant.'

'An accountant? Was that something you were going to do?'

'No, but my dad's a lawyer and he somehow expected me to follow in his footsteps so, stupidly, I said I'd rather be an accountant and they took it seriously. It was one sarcastic comment, but they are clinging on to that possibility and they mention it every time I visit.'

'But they know you have a business with your paintings, don't they? Surely they can appreciate how you've dedicated yourself to that and understand how much it means to you?'

'I think they do, but only as a hobby. They just don't see it as a real job, at least not the kind of job they want to tell their neighbours about.'

'Hmm. They always want something to brag about, I think. Certainly, they would probably be proud to say their son is an accountant, but that doesn't mean their neighbour would think the same way. My impression of accountants is that they are boring and too straight to have any fun, so if the neighbour feels the same it wouldn't be anything to brag about. Maybe their neighbour is an art lover himself, or has a much less academic lifestyle which would be considerably more receptive to news of a creative career. Their opinion of a real job isn't necessarily the same as someone else's, so it might be time to let them know they need to support your choice, which is definitely real to you.'

'You're probably right,' Panos agreed. 'It's just been easier to ignore it so far and just fob them off when I visit, but if it's going to be an ongoing conversation every time I see them, it's time I put them straight. I'm getting some regular commissions now, so although I prefer to keep my finances private, if I tell them what I'm currently earning it should shock them into silence.'

'A decent salary then?' Theo asked with barely hidden surprise.

'Now that my name is getting known and my agent has contacts with the kind of people who appreciate my work, it's going very well,' he smiled modestly.

'Good for you,' Theo said honestly and with only a trace of jealousy. 'It must be nice to make a living doing something you enjoy.'

'It's an absolute dream and I know everyone isn't so lucky.'

'Well, my job isn't a dream but I do enjoy it. Mostly.' Theo said carefully.

'I can see that you really enjoy talking to the customers and finding out what they've been doing on their holiday. I get more locals on my stall and I do like a little conversation, but I don't know if I could cope with some of the craziness the tourists often bring into the market.'

'It can be a real laugh,' Theo replied genuinely, 'and most of the time they're just having fun. You do get to meet all sorts though.'

'What was that woman doing the other day? The one who was getting undressed in the middle of the market?'

'She insisted on trying on one of those sarongs which wrap around the arms and stay on without having to be tied, but she couldn't do it over her top, so she just whipped it off without any warning!' Theo laughed as he remembered his surprise.

'When I looked over to see what all the noise was about, all I could see was a woman waving her arms around in nothing but a bikini top.'

'She wasn't embarrassed at all and she certainly didn't have the smallest boobs I've ever seen.'

'She was quite a large lady,' Panos recalled, with a grimace. 'It's not the kind of thing you expect to see in the market place.'

'It's not, but in her defence, she'd probably just spent the previous few hours sitting in a beach bar chatting to everyone who passed in just a teeny-weeny bikini and not feeling uncomfortable at all.'

'You're probably right. I don't get to see much of the tourists at play because I don't really go to those areas when I'm not working. It's only in here that I actually meet some of the island's visitors.'

'You're missing a trick there,' Theo pointed out. 'I'm always in the bars at night and it's so much fun watching them cut loose and do whatever they want. You can get a real sense of freedom from observing them in action and it's easy to get swept up in the enjoyment of the moment.'

'Sounds like you should be working in the bars, rather than a quiet stall in the market,' Panos observed.

'But then I'd be limited to how much I could join in if I was working. I prefer having fun there in my own time and having the chance to chat to them properly when they come to buy their souvenirs, although…'

'Go on,' Panos prompted as Theo hesitated.

'Well, I've often thought how much I'd like to spend more time talking to them and telling them more about the island itself, so that they really understand the history in some of the souvenirs they buy.'

'You mean, like doing an organised presentation or something?'

'Not quite, although maybe…' Theo tried to put together the random thoughts he'd been having into some kind of order so that he could pinpoint exactly what he was searching for.

'You would probably have to do it outside of the market though,' Panos wondered.

'Exactly! Yes! That's what I want to do,' Theo exclaimed. 'I hadn't really thought it through properly, but I would love to take people to the actual locations of the ornaments I sell and explain the history of each one.'

'Don't the tour companies do that already?'

'I suppose they do…' Theo considered that fact for a while with a thoughtful frown and Panos gave him the time to work through what he was weighing up. 'But they do a full island tour with visits to honey farms and scenic photo opportunities and I would stay more local with the emphasis specifically on historic events.'

'And that's something you really want to do?'

'I think so. I've had some thoughts about doing a bit more than just selling souvenirs, but I haven't really put it into words until today,' he shrugged. 'I guess I've got some thinking to do.'

'Sounds like you and Selina both have ideas about where you'd prefer to be working. Maybe you could support each other to finally give it a go,' Panos suggested.

'Selina?'

'You know, with the olive oil production.' Panos tried to remember if she had told him about her ultimate dream in secret, but even if that was the case, Theo was her partner and would have to have known about it.

'She told you about that? I thought she'd forgotten all about it since she decided she didn't want to leave the island. I know she really liked the idea, but there's no way she can do it here and she's happy enough with the stall anyway.'

'Right.' Panos knew for a fact that Selina had not given up on her dream as she had mentioned it more than once, but realised she must have told Theo that she had. It didn't bode well for their relationship if she had to pretend that she was happy with the way things were and sacrifice her dream job, just because she wasn't getting the support she needed. He could see that Theo had plans of his own to consider, so it was up to him to find a way to help Selina to move forward with her career aspirations. He had a couple of ideas, but there was no rush as it was still a few months from olive-picking season, so he had time to research some of the best options.

'Hey, I wonder if Rosie could give me a few tips on doing an organised tour? She's often said she wishes she could just go with her own schedule sometimes instead of being stuck to the official plan all the time. She might have some ideas about how I might be able to do it in a fun way.'

'She probably would; she always seems to enjoy chatting to the groups she brings in and I'm sure she must get a lot of feedback from them about things they want to see,' Panos agreed.

'She's the ideal woman,' Theo nodded. They both knew what he meant, but Theo felt a little guilty after making the comment, and Panos' reaction to hearing those words was to form a mental image of Selina. 'I'll have a word with her once I've tidied up the last of this food and binned all the rubbish.'

'Do you want a hand?'

'No, you're a guest so you should be relaxing. I'll get Selina to help out and then maybe we can all have another beer together before I set up the games.'

Theo and Selina made light work of the clearing and tidying, but they had an ideal opportunity to discuss something that was on her mind.

'I think Rosie's a bit lonely. We were talking earlier and I get the impression she'd like a bit of romance in her life.'

'Did she say that?' Theo asked in surprise. He knew that Rosie had never mentioned how she felt about a new boyfriend, but she never gave the impression she was looking. He was a little uncomfortable with the feeling that she might be looking.

'No one ever says that, silly. She just made me feel like she was missing out after her break up and that romance was important to her.'

'Well, I suppose she'll meet someone when she's ready,' Theo shrugged. He didn't think she was ready yet. He wasn't even sure if he was ready for her to be ready yet.

'But I think she is ready. And I know the perfect solution.'

'You do? Why am I asking? Of course you do.' Selina always had the perfect solution; he should have known that by now.

'Any other year I might have been struggling, but this year we've been gifted with the answer.'

'So who's your ideal candidate?'

'You make it sound so formal, but they already know each other. She won't think of Panos as being the ideal candidate, she'll think he's hot to trot!'

'Panos? Isn't he a bit…'

'A bit what?'

'I don't know. Square?'

'What on earth do you mean? He's lovely looking, he looks after himself and he knows how to have a meaningful conversation.'

'I thought Leandra was after him?'

'I've managed to keep her away for now; he deserves better than that,' Selina huffed.

'But I can't imagine them together,' Theo insisted.

'Why not? They're both single, they're not looking for anything serious after their break ups and we could even start off on a double date to put them at ease.'

'I don't know.' Theo couldn't imagine going on a double date with anyone, but to have to watch someone fawning all over Rosie actually made him feel queasy.

'Well, I do, so once the games are over and we can relax a bit, I'm going to sit them together and we'll see how long it takes for nature to takes its course,' she grinned.

'If you say so,' he said, shaking his head. He could only hope that nature intervened a little bit sooner and tired everyone out so much during the games that they could hardly be bothered to join in any conversation afterwards.

Selina helped Panos over to a nearby sunbed and made him sit there until she returned with two bottles of water.

'Sip this, slowly,' she instructed him.

'I'm OK really, just a little woozy. I haven't played that game before.'

'Theo should know better, after everyone's been drinking his homemade cocktails. Constantly spinning around a basketball will make you dizzy at any time of the day, but it's a hundred times worse after alcohol.'

'I think that was the idea,' Panos said, as he sipped the water with his eyes closed to avoid the vision of swirling colours.

'Well it was a bad one. I've told him to wind things down now because most people would prefer a leisurely nap to chasing up and down the beach all afternoon.'

'I'm not sure I could lie down right now. I'm happy just to sit here and chat.'

'Just as well because I told Theo to join us and he's bringing Rosie so she's not on her own.'

'In that case, before they get here, do you think I could ask you a favour?'

'Fire away,' she smiled.

'I've had a request for a particular landscape and I've got a place in mind, but I think it would be more striking if I had someone standing at the side, taking in the view themselves.'

'So you're looking for a model?'

'Well, not a professional model, just someone with their back to me, appreciating the view. I wondered if that could be you?'

'You want to paint me?' she said with surprise and a slight case of butterflies.

'Officially, yes, but no one will know it's you. It depends really if you have time, or if you've already got plans because I would need to do it on a Sunday so that I've got the whole day to capture the best colours. I usually take lots of photographs so that I can finish the piece at home once I've got all the basics in place, so if you even had time to come along for me to get some pictures of you at the scene that would be very helpful.'

'But it would be better if I was there as you were painting, wouldn't it?'

'It would feel more realistic, but you can't hang around all day.'

'Why not? I keep Sundays free for relaxing and that sounds like a wonderful way to do that. I wouldn't need to paste on any make up if my face isn't showing so I wouldn't be uncomfortable, as long as we can take breaks for the bathroom and refreshments.'

'Yes, I take regular breaks or it becomes too intense, but do you think you'd be able to cope with a full day? I'd be happy with an hour or two if you can manage that.'

'Well let's say I'll come with you so that you can get whatever details you need and then if I want to leave it won't be a problem, but also, if I stay after that it might be a nice day for both of us.'

'What might be a nice day?' Theo asked as he arrived with Rosie.

'I'm going to help Panos out with something for his art collection. It'll be on a Sunday which means no doubt you'll be in bed with a hangover, so I may as well help him out while you're sleeping it off.'

'That's what Sundays are for in my book,' Theo laughed and Rosie joined in.

'Ooh I love a lie-in on a Sunday, but when I was in Kefalos I lived near to a church and it was agony trying to hide under the pillow to deafen the sound of the bells. Never again.'

'We'll have to make sure there are no churches near to any flats you check out around here then,' Theo suggested.

'You're coming to live in Kos Town?' Selina asked. 'That will be great; you'll be able to join in with more of our get togethers, although you'd be forgiven for excusing yourself from another mad afternoon like this.'

'Oh, I've had so much fun today!' Rosie beamed. 'Thank you again for inviting me, it's been a real laugh.'

'I knew you'd have a good time,' Theo said as he playfully nudged her with his elbow. 'I hope you do move here because I know we could win the three-legged race next time.'

'We'll see; it depends on price and location. I don't mind if it's quite small, even just a studio, but I would prefer to be in town rather than on the outskirts and if that's too expensive then I'll probably have to pass.'

'Maybe Panos could help you look for somewhere?' Selina suggested. 'You must have checked out a few places when you first came over?'

'I did look at a few, but I was needed around the house while my grandfather recovered and it was easier and cheaper to stay there.'

'But now he's recovering well isn't he, so maybe you could look for a two-bed flat and share as room-mates? That would make things cheaper for you both and you already know each other, so that could be the perfect solution,' Selina grinned as though she had struck gold.

'I've already said I'll give Rosie a hand to find some available rooms,' Theo said eagerly. 'You don't need to worry Panos about searching through the listings.'

'But it might work out for both of them in the end. Anyway,' Selina said as she linked arms with Theo, 'you said you would help me with that *thing* once the games were done, so?'

'What thing? Can't I just relax for a bit?' Theo had enjoyed his day, but even he was ready for a rest.

'Ha, men never remember things, do they?' she laughed as she began to pull Theo away. 'Anyway, we won't be long, so maybe you two can work out a time when you're both free to get together for a coffee or something and check out what accommodation is available around the town? Panos, maybe you could get the taxi back to Kardamena with Rosie and enjoy a meal somewhere different while you discuss your options? Theo, come on,' she insisted as he reluctantly followed her lead.

'Oh, do you need someone to take you back tonight?' Panos asked considerately. 'I'm not sure I'm up for a late night after that last game.'

'No, really, it's fine. I wasn't going to leave for a good while yet so when I do, I'll probably have a drink on the main strip here first then just go straight home to bed.'

'Yes, I think I heard Theo say a few of them are going to Bar Street once it gets dark, so at least you won't be on your own.'

'We were going to work out when he's free to show me around a few places, but if you're looking for somewhere too, we can arrange it so we're all available at the same time.'

'I'm not sure why Selina thought I might want to move out; I'm not paying rent as I'm taking care of the house and the household bills are much cheaper between three of us, so I don't really need to leave. If I was thinking of living here permanently it would be a different matter, but it's only for one summer and I'm fine where I am.'

'That's good because I really wasn't looking for somewhere to share. I was sharing with my boyfriend for three years and the last few months I've been in my mate's spare room, so I'm ready to enjoy the space in a place of my own for now, just until I work out my next move.'

'It's probably just as well that Theo has offered to help then, because he'll have a much better idea about what kind of places are available and what you should be paying for each type.'

'He's been ever so kind and helpful. When I first started to bring the tours into the market place, I really wasn't sure if I would last the season because I felt so lost, being suddenly on my own, but he soon made me feel welcome and he's so funny; he always makes me laugh.'

'I can believe it because I felt exactly the same, being thrown in the deep end with my grandfather's flower business. I wasn't really sure what to do and I didn't think I'd be able to pull it off, but everyone at the market has been so supportive and Selina is always on hand with some worthwhile advice to make things run more smoothly.'

'They really are a lovely couple, aren't they?' Rosie pondered.

'Absolutely,' Panos agreed. 'They've really gone to town today to make sure everyone has fun and feels like part of a team and at the same time, they know us individually enough to have those personal conversations which make all the difference.'

'They've made all the difference to me,' Rosie concurred, thinking about how Theo had brightened up her life in a way she couldn't have imagined.

'Me too,' Panos nodded, thinking how Selina was, in more than a hundred ways, more different than any other woman he had ever met.

They sat with their individual thoughts as they gazed out to sea and gradually nodded off in a haze of contentment.

AUGUST

Early one Sunday morning, Panos collected Selina in his grandfather's old Toyota and, after apologising for the lack of air conditioning, they set off for a peaceful but creative day.

They followed the coastal road away from the town towards the edge of the mountainous region, which passed several all-inclusive hideaways before coming to an abrupt end at the thermal springs. Around this side of the island, Turkey once again appeared close enough to touch, but it was no longer the tourism-heavy little whitewashed villages easily visible from the harbour which were in evidence here, but rough and uncompromising cliffs with a formidable headland. Dramatic wasn't the word. It looked exactly like something out of a pirate movie, throwing out a distinct challenge to be conquered along with an undeniable air of mystery. It was perfect for the scene Panos had in mind and the challenge for him was not to climb the cliff with its element of danger, but to accurately capture its true spirit along with its hidden vulnerability of loneliness on the canvas, so that the viewer would feel in touch with all those emotions simultaneously.

On such a perfect summer day, the intermittent colours visible during their journey, powerfully contrasted against each other. Every so often there would be a group of pink or red flowers, which stood proud from the scorched and sandy earth below and it was a miracle they'd had the opportunity to grow in such dry conditions, but nature was renowned for its tenacity. At one particular bend in the road, there stood a derelict tower which had partially collapsed but was rumoured to have once acted as an ancient lighthouse. Its terracotta bricks had been bleached by the sun and appeared even brighter against a backdrop of the cerulean sea it guarded. Further along the road, the uniformly small bright white blocks of accommodation in the all-inclusive hotels seemed at odds to be sandwiched between the natural sapphire blue of the sky and the obligatory turquoise of the Olympic-sized swimming pool. The final part of the road was absent of any colourful distractions, but none were needed as the eye automatically looked out from the high vantage point over the coastline for the grand finale. The only thing between the cliff top at the edge of the roadside and the cliff top on the neighbouring headland of Turkey, was a current of swirling patterns in every shade of blue, displaying the true power of the sea a few hundred feet below.

Panos parked in a designated lay-by and they both sat looking at the view in silence for a few moments; even the locals never got bored of this view and the tourists could never understand how it wasn't more generally promoted. It took some time for the human brain to catch up with the unexpected emotions the scene aroused, but it was an experience which was never forgotten in a hurry.

'Now I understand why you wanted me to wear white,' Selina said, quite breathlessly.

'The colours out there are so pure, it's the only option,' Panos nodded.

They didn't want to break the spell by walking into the scene before them, chatting and organising how it was all going to work but the car, even with its open windows, was beginning to overheat and so they had no choice.

Panos pointed out a nearby tree where she could wait in the shade and where he planned to arrange all his artistic essentials. Unfortunately, the tree was not at all picturesque, nor in the correct location, because he would have liked to have constructed the vision of a solitary windswept spectacle overlooking such a wonderfully natural vista, but he knew that by having Selina as the silent observer, the viewer of the finished item would immediately become immersed in her world and that was always the unspoken challenge of a perfect piece of art.

Once all the pencils, paints, sketch books and canvas were prepared and ready for use, Panos asked Selina to stand in a few different positions and took photographs of the scene to get an idea of the best angles where he could capture the most colour contrasts.

She had brought a large sunhat, but it had such a floppy brim that the wind kept ruffling it, threatening to blow it off and over the edge of the cliff to the sea below.

'Do you have anything I could pin it with?' she asked hopefully. 'I'm guessing if I hold it, that will spoil the effect of a calm atmosphere, but I haven't got anything I can secure it with.'

'Mmm. I don't think so. I hadn't really thought it through.' He was slightly annoyed that his plans hadn't included how to secure a loose hat, but he was impressed that Selina understood that holding it wouldn't create the right effect.

'I've only got a small cap instead, but that really won't work,' she laughed. 'What if I held it on, but you didn't draw my hand, then I can take it off and you can complete it with my arms more naturally?'

'Maybe.' He was thinking through another possibility. 'Would you mind if we did this without the hat? Your hair looks lovely in that plait, so it would be nice to show it, if it's not too intrusive?'

'Well, I put it up like this because I knew it would be a bit breezy and you don't want loads of hair flying around. Leandra taught me how to do it once and it's been quite useful sometimes. I guess I don't mind, but you didn't want my face to be on it so can you avoid that?'

'It's not that I didn't want your face to be on it, but the customer has asked specifically for a landscape view so it would be a distraction if there's a beautiful face taking away the attention.'

Oops, that was too much information.

'Oh! Well, erm, if I'm looking out to sea, you should only get the back of my head anyway, so as long as you're OK with that I'm happy to be hatless.' She tried to ignore what his words had done to her stomach, but it was an unusual feeling and she quite liked it.

'I think that would look more natural, but apart from when I'm actually concentrating on your hair, maybe you should wear the cap to keep the sun off your head. We'll have regular breaks, but you don't want to overdo it.'

'Good idea. Are we ready to get started?'

'I just need a few more photos and then I'll sketch the outline, then I'll finalise your position and mark it so we don't lose the spot when we take a break.'

'Just let me know what you need me to do; I'm in your hands,' she said with a smile and both of them secretly felt a warm glow from the suggestion.

The situation was very unusual for Selina because, as he was working, Panos was completely silent, concentrating on the shape and colour and movement which he was trying to reproduce. At the same time, she was gazing out over the spectacular view in front of her and wondering how nature managed to be so perfect. She couldn't imagine how Panos would be able to recreate the colours she was seeing because they looked completely original and they often formed hues that she was sure she had never seen before. She was certain that most of them didn't have an official shade that you could buy as a paint colour and she could only hope that her friend had enough talent to be able to combine two or three to get anywhere close to the magical kaleidoscope of the real thing.

After some time in their own thoughts, it took a little while for conversation to flow on their short breaks. They had brought some cheese pies and stuffed vine leaves, along with a small salad and plenty of water.

'I was going to bring some wine, but I thought you might get a bit dehydrated in this heat and I don't drink while I'm working,' Panos explained.

'I don't like drinking during the day anyway, particularly in this heat. I might have one or two with dinner sometimes, but only if I'm out, otherwise it's probably just the occasional beer at home.'

'I thought you and Theo liked going out to parties and clubs.'

'Theo loves it! He's been the same ever since we left school; he loves to be the life and soul of any events we get invited to and he's out most weekends, until dawn sometimes. I just don't see the point. I like dancing and chatting with everyone, but I suppose it's because I don't drink that much, once they all start getting a bit noisy, I just make my excuses and go home.'

'I suppose the night scene isn't for everyone, particularly the way it works here where it's party time every night.'

'I'd rather have an early start than a late night, any day of the week,' she said thoughtfully.

'I'm the same, as long as it's not too early. I've been up at sunrise on the odd occasion, but any earlier than that wouldn't suit me. Years ago, my parents took me on an African safari when I was just a boy and we were getting up at something like 3 or 4 in the morning! I carried on sleeping, curled up under a blanket in the jeep, until the sun came up and we reached the main areas.'

'That must have been amazing! I would love to do that.'

'It probably was amazing, but not for a teenage boy; I had other priorities at that stage of my life,' he laughed. 'I definitely think it takes an adult to appreciate that kind of experience.'

'I think sunrise is the best part of the day,' Selina said with a warm smile. 'It just seems to inspire me and give me hope that the coming day will be full of wonderful opportunities.'

Panos was nodding with an appreciation of her revelation, but then he heard what her words might actually be implying and his expression became a worried frown. 'Do you *need* that hope to fill your day with wonderful opportunities? Don't you have lots to look forward to anyway, without needing the hope of an inspirational sunrise?'

'Well, I suppose so. I mean, I'm happy with my life, but I'm open to any little surprise that the day might want to throw my way. It's not like I use each sunrise to wish for some secret dream, but any morning that I'm lucky enough to see the gorgeous spectacle, I hope it will bring a little luck into my life.'

'So, if it were to bring you some luck, what kind of thing would you like to be surprised with?'

'I've no idea. Like I said, it's not a wish for something in particular, it's more like a hope for a good day. Maybe Leandra will tell me that a film I'm interested in has been scheduled in at the cinema, or I'll see an unexpected rainbow, or Theo will surprise me with some ice cream, or someone will post an advert for staff to help with their olive picking requirements.'

'And those things would make you feel like the sunrise has given you a little bit of magic?'

'Maybe. Except for the ice cream. Theo always gets two tubs of his favourite flavour, but I don't really like it so he usually finishes it for me anyway,' she shrugged.

'I see.' He didn't see at all. Firstly, he would hope that Selina had everything in her life which made her as happy as she could be, not expecting a morning vision to be inspirational enough to create something to fill the missing gaps. Secondly, she had mentioned the olive picking business again and he knew that was something she was interested in, but for some reason she was prepared to ignore her own desires and give in to family expectations. Lastly, why on earth would Theo buy a flavour of ice cream that she didn't like? From what Selina had said, she wasn't a massive ice cream fan anyway, so that was just a double fault of laziness on his part and unforgiveable for someone who was supposed to be in a loving relationship.

'Are you happy with how I look?' she asked suddenly.

'Wha…? Yes, you look lovely,' he stammered, wondering if she was reading his mind about how he genuinely felt about her.

'I mean on the painting,' she laughed. 'Do you want me to do anything different because I don't mind changing position if it helps with the ambience.'

'No, I like what you're doing. I mean,' he began again, 'I like your position in the shot. The colour is going to start changing now throughout the afternoon so I'll take some more photos and decide which will be the best time frame to base the images on. The headland will get a lot darker as the sun starts to dip so that might be the best option for that area, but the colours of the sea will begin to merge so that's not as good. I need to capture the best light for each object, but still make sure it all looks like the same time of the day.'

'I really didn't realise it was so complicated. I thought you just set up your easel and drew what you could see.'

'It can be that way with a portrait or a still life but anything outdoors, or in nature, has a specific movement and colour change that can only be represented honestly over a period of time. Sometimes that can be just a day, but sometimes, particularly in the observation of plants and trees, it needs to be days, or even weeks.'

'I can understand that. I've seen such a change in personality with the olive trees over the course of a year, so a painting of the same tree six months apart would look like a completely different object.'

'That's right,' he agreed wholeheartedly. He loved how she was beginning to understand his passion and how there was a deeper level of involvement than many people realised. He also loved the flash of a mental image of him painting her as she stood under one of those olive trees.

'Should we get back to it then?' she asked as she screwed on the lid of the water bottle she had just emptied in an eager gulp.

'If you're ready?' he nodded.

'I can't wait,' she giggled. 'I'm having a brilliant time.'

He was glad to hear her words of assurance, as they moved back to the focal point. He wasn't sure exactly what was missing in her life, but he was glad he was bringing that little spark of hope and inspiration to her day and decided that he wanted to be just like the sunrise she treasured, to shine a bit of magic on her hopes and dreams for the future.

On the same Sunday afternoon, Theo was helping Rosie to find her way around some of the apartments which were advertised for rent.

'This one does have a nice private balcony,' Rosie observed at their third stop. 'At least if I don't get along with the neighbours, I won't have to feel obliged to make polite conversation.'

'But it's facing north so you'll never really get any sunshine on it. If that's what you want.'

'Hmm. I'd rather go to the beach to sunbathe, rather than in the middle of town like this, but it might be nice to have the option of a bit of sunshine now and then.'

'There are no wardrobes in here again, though,' Theo observed as he looked inside the drawers and cupboards. 'There's a manky old fridge, but no hob or cooking utensils, so I think that's why it's a bit cheaper than the others and probably more suited to a local with family to borrow from.'

'Well at least it's got its own bathroom,' she noted as she opened, then quickly closed the bathroom door, with a grimace. 'I couldn't believe people would still rent rooms without private facilities like the last place we went to. As if I'm going to stand in the corridor with my legs crossed waiting for someone to shave their face, or their legs, before I can spend a penny!'

'And it cost more than a penny to rent, even though it was suspiciously cheaper than the others,' Theo nodded.

'I really don't think I'm going to find anywhere within my price range in the middle of town. It would be convenient, but it's definitely not worth the cost if I have to go and buy all the things that make life a bit more comfortable.'

'There are more to look at on the outskirts, but we'd need to stick to the local bus route, unless you get a moped, or a bicycle.'

'I'm happy to walk if I find something in the local area, but if it's further afield I wouldn't mind using a bicycle. My ex had one I would sometimes borrow to get to the other side of Kefalos, but obviously it was useless going up the hills at either end of the resort.'

'I can imagine, although I've seen many tourists try it. Can't say I'm keen on making that much effort when a moped would zoom up there in no time. One of those electric bicycles would be helpful though.'

'But if I do move to Kos Town, the whole place is as flat as a pancake, so that would never be an issue. It might also be quite nice to use the cycle path along the shoreline and making the most of the view on my way to work.'

'Just watch out for the tourists who've never been here before, because they seem to think it's some kind of walkway and always think the bikes should go around them, instead of getting out of the way and letting the cyclists go ahead to use their own special lane.'

'Oh, I saw some kind of kerfuffle near the castle when I was doing the tour the other day. It's really narrow just around the bridge and there was a bit of shouting and tinkling of bells, but the group blocking the way just carried on regardless.'

'Yes, it can be a bit tricky where the path narrows, but if everyone just used their common sense it wouldn't be such an obstacle.'

'Now you're asking,' she laughed. 'Common sense? On holiday? I think that's asking a bit too much, in my experience.'

'And this place is asking too much for no storage or cooking facilities. Let's move on.'

They visited a few more places, but for every plus point there were at least two negatives and none of them were at a price which Rosie could comfortably afford on her own.

'There are two more possibilities,' Theo said as he checked his information. 'One is a little out of the way and it's just a small studio and the other is an en-suite room in a shared house. Both are under your budget, but from what we've seen I'm not holding out much hope of either of them being a dream home.'

'No, I don't expect I'm going to find a dream home, but somewhere clean and fairly up-to-date would be just fine. Let's give them a try and keep our fingers crossed.'

The first place was a little off the beaten track, with a very rough and winding pathway which seemed to go on forever.

'I'm not sure I'd want to be coming home to this place on my own in the dark,' Rosie said nervously. 'It's quite pretty in the sunlight, but I don't see any lights to guide the way at night.'

'No, but it's not like you'd need to be scared about someone jumping out on you. That kind of thing just doesn't happen here.'

'Maybe not, but it would still be scary, even if a dog jumped out. I'd be more worried about snakes.'

'You might have a point,' Theo agreed, as they followed the last curve in the path to arrive at a tiny white building with the remains of a vegetable patch outside. 'Ah.'

'Indeed. Is that a farmer's hut?' she asked with astonishment.

'Very possibly. It's obviously been renovated, but I'm not sure what the facilities will be like.'

'I suppose we should have a look now that we're here,' she said without much enthusiasm.

'I really don't think this is for you, but I'm curious to see what it's like,' he said, as they went over to peer through the window.

'Well, it's surprisingly cleaner than I expected, but it really is tiny.'

'That's because half of it is round the back,' Theo shouted from the rear of the building.

'What the hell?' she laughed as she saw the al-fresco bathroom unit, with a dilapidated wooden screen to protect the user's privacy, almost doubling the total floor space.

'This is definitely not for you,' Theo declared, torn between laughing along with Rosie and being annoyed that someone could actually think this was a useful space for anyone but a farmer.

'I don't really think it's for anyone, unless someone out there is desperate to get back to nature, without having to leave the island. Nice and secluded for a hermit though,' she smiled cheekily.

'Come on, let's try the last place. I've called ahead so there'll be someone waiting to show us around.'

They couldn't help giggling and describing the kind of person who would want to live in the farmer's hut, all the way to the next apartment.

They left the main road and followed the directions to pass a couple of small self-catering units and venture a little further up the hill to a builder's yard, from which the house stood directly opposite.

'This looks nice,' Rosie smiled. 'And look at the view!'

'What? A builder's yard?'

'No. Back there,' she nodded as she indicated the scene behind Theo's head.

'Of course, we're high enough here to get a good view over the harbour and across to Turkey. It always surprises me how different it looks from up here rather than when I'm scooting around the town in and out of the one-way system.'

'It really is gorgeous.'

'Well, it's nice to get a good perspective, but it's hardly as picturesque as Kefalos. You've been spoiled a bit there,' Theo observed.

'Yes, I do miss that view,' she admitted, swallowing an unexpected wobble. She did miss it, but only because she'd always seen it with *him*. Any view was better shared with someone else, but when there was no one to share it with, it didn't have quite the same effect. The truth was, she was missing someone to share things with more than she was missing the familiarity of the place she'd had to leave. She could go and visit the sights whenever she wanted to, but just how long it would be before she had someone to enjoy that experience with, she had no idea and that made her sad.

'Oops, sorry, I shouldn't have brought that up. We're looking forward now, aren't we?' he said, as he smiled that irresistible smile. 'So, let's go and look at this room because I've got a good feeling about it.'

'Me too,' she nodded.

The house was on two levels with a reception room, a study and a kitchen on the ground floor which was for general use between everyone. There was a small terrace behind with some chairs and a table, but it wasn't open to the view of the harbour they had just enjoyed as it backed onto another building, which looked like some kind of storage unit.

There were four bedrooms upstairs and the vacant one was on the front of the building, again with no spectacular view, unless there were going to be any young and attractive builders in the yard opposite.

'I'll let you have a look around yourselves, then just meet me downstairs again when you're ready,' the possible new housemate suggested.

'There's a lot of space down there,' Theo pointed out. 'I don't think you'd ever feel crowded.'

'No, it's nice.'

'You've got all the pots and pans you'd need and plenty of seating options.'

'Yes, that's good.'

'And up here you've got loads of cupboards and wardrobe space. I know women generally have a lot more stuff than me, but I still think you've got plenty of room.'

'You're right, it's got everything I need.'

'So, the rent is manageable, even with the extras you'd pay for the basic foodstuffs and necessities that everyone shares. I hadn't actually thought about things like salt and sugar, or washing up liquid and fabric softener. I suppose they've got a good system in place, so you wouldn't have to try and work all that out for yourself.'

'It does seem like everything is taken care of.'

'I guess it is up a bit of a hill, if you're cycling, but it's not that far, so you could just walk the last section in five or ten minutes.'

'It would be a handy bit of weight-bearing exercise, at least.'

'So, you like it?'

'It does seem to be just what I need. I wonder, would you mind leaving me here for a few minutes? I think I need to see how it feels when it's just me on my own.'

'Oh, of course. I'll go down and see if I can find out if they subscribe to any satellite channels.'

'Thanks,' she smiled, as she closed the door behind him.

She leaned against the door and almost allowed herself to release the tears which she had been trying so hard to hold back, but knew she couldn't hide the bloodshot eyes and swollen face which it would create. She gulped in rapid mouthfuls of oxygen and tried to look away from the double bed which had started the whole emotional disturbance in the first place.

The last time she'd slept in a double bed, she'd been in a happy relationship with a promising future ahead of her or, at least, that was what she had believed. For the last few months, she'd been sleeping in her friend's spare single bed and it had reinforced the fact that this would be her life for the moment, unless she did something about it. Now she was faced with a new life and a new place to live, with a double bed, but was she actually ready to share it with anyone?

She blew her nose and cleared her throat to rebalance her senses, but it didn't shift the thought that the first thing she'd imagined when she saw it, was Theo's nakedness inviting her to join him there. It had been difficult to speak to him when she was imagining what they could be doing together between those welcoming white sheets. She'd known she fancied him since they first met, but now they seemed to be getting closer and it was more difficult to ignore, so that when she thought of her future and who she might get together with, it was impossible to think of anyone but him.

The room, and the whole house, seemed perfect for her, but if she did move to Kos Town, there would be a lot more opportunities to socialise and Theo was bound to be around all the time with his party-loving ways. Last month, she might have thought that would be a nice treat for her, but now she realised it would be an absolute torment and something she really couldn't bear. It was time she put a stop to this silly infatuation and remove herself from the wonderful group of friends that she had so much wanted to become a part of. It hurt too much to be near the one person she wanted and couldn't have.

'Thank you,' she said as she walked straight past the friendly tenant and Theo, who was looking through a huge selection of DVDs. 'We've got somewhere else to see and then I'll be in touch if I want to come back.'

'Erm, thanks,' Theo echoed in a hurry as he followed her out.

'Can you just drop me at the bus station? I don't feel great all of a sudden.'

'Oh no, what's wrong? Do you need more water? Are you too hot?'

'No, I've got water thanks, I just feel a bit stressed about everything. You know, it's a big decision to move up to Kos Town. I don't think I'm ready for it,' she offered as an excuse.

'It must be a huge thing to come to terms with,' he agreed as they sat in the car, sipping their drinks. 'First you have to suffer through a break up and then move to a completely new place…'

'In my friend's spare room.'

'Yes, not even a space you can call your own. I guess you'd be scared to move out of there for something that might be no better but, I have to say, I really think this place is great. You probably need to mull it over for a bit, but I wouldn't take too long because I don't think it will be free for long.'

'You're right, but I do need to think things over, so I'll get out of your hair now and make my way home.'

'I don't think that's a good idea. You need to talk things through and maybe we can work out what's holding you back so that we can make this happen.'

'I'm not sure I'm ready to talk about it yet,' she said, a little too quickly. The things she needed to think over were not the things she could talk to Theo about.

'OK, so let's do something physical so that we don't have to think at all.'

'Sorry?' Rosie wasn't sure how that word had escaped her lips when her brain was in a complete spin about what Theo could mean.

'Let's go for a swim. We said we might do that if we had time. You did bring your beach stuff?' he asked needlessly, as her canvas bag was clearly full of all the necessary items.

'Well, yes, but…'

'No buts. If you need to de-stress, we can forget the talking and just listen to the radio while we go down to the beach, then have a swim and wash all our cares away.'

'That does sound good,' she agreed, 'but I'm not sure I want to be surrounded by screaming kids and noisy volleyball players. She didn't often swim, but it did sound like something which might help her to calm down, if it wasn't a busy area.

'I know the perfect place,' he said and switched on the radio as they set off on a much more relaxing journey.

As they travelled out of the town and along some roads Rosie had never seen before, she thought over what she needed to come to terms with. She would have to distance herself from Theo and that would be painful because she had completely fallen for him, but she wasn't a home wrecker and he wouldn't be interested anyway. This would be the last time she would let herself be close to him, so she decided to enjoy his company for the afternoon and let herself dream, just for a little while, then get back to reality and consider returning to Ireland at the end of the season.

Theo could see that Rosie had been stressed by the thought of moving again to a new resort, but he believed it would be good for her to be closer to people she could call friends and he really enjoyed having her around. He was hoping to ask her about his idea of doing small tours around the town to explain the history behind some of the souvenirs he sold and looked forward to the possibility of her offering to help him set it up. When they'd viewed the last property, he'd realised that he also had a spare room he could rent out for a little extra cash and toyed with the idea of offering it to Rosie, but something about it didn't seem quite right and he knew he had to check it out with Selina first, as she spent more and more time in there.

He pulled in at the side of the road, where there seemed to be no facilities and no beach.

'Have you run out of petrol,' Rosie teased.

'No, this is my favourite, out of the way, hidden beach.'

'This?' she asked, pointing to the road ahead.

'No, this,' he said as he took her hand and made his way through a gap in the thicket, over a couple of boulders and down a slight incline of slippery pebbles, to show her a very small and secluded bay.

'Oh My God! That is beautiful. Are you the only one who knows it's here?' she asked in amazement.

'I doubt it, but I've never bumped into anyone else while I've been here. It's my special hideaway.'

'Won't Selina mind that you've brought me to your special place?'

'She doesn't know about it. It's where I come to get some space from reality.'

'Oh.' Rosie was surprised that he hadn't taken his girlfriend to such a wonderful place, but more so that he needed a place to get away from her. That didn't sound like true love at all.

'Come on, I'm desperate for a swim,' he said as he stripped down to his shorts in no time and threw himself beneath the surface.

Rosie undressed a little more calmly and gradually waded in up to her thighs before lowering herself gently into the calm water.

They both enjoyed their swim and then chatted on the beach while they dried off. Rosie had a few ideas about Theo's plan to do his small tours and found herself volunteering to help out, despite her decision to stay out of his way.

After a while, she asked if Selina would be expecting him back soon, but he explained how Panos had asked for her help with creating some kind of art, so they had plenty of time.

'He's only here for the summer, I think,' Rosie said.

'Yes. He'll be heading back to the mainland in autumn. Did you know Selina was trying to fix you up with him?'

'Was she? He's really nice and I enjoy talking to him, but we don't have any kind of chemistry.'

'So you don't think you could be more than friends?' Theo asked unexpectedly.

'Well, he's very handsome so I suppose if things were different, we could have been friends with benefits,' she giggled.

'Like us, you mean?'

'Oh,' she almost squealed. 'Is that what we are?' She had forgotten everything she'd previously decided about staying away from him; how could she possibly do that? Was he actually saying that he wanted what she wanted?

'I think so. We're friends, aren't we?'

'I hope so,' she murmured.

'And we enjoy doing the same kind of things, so that's definitely a benefit.'

'I guess so…'

'Of course it is! We're friends with benefits because we like doing loads of the same things and we always have fun when we're together. It's brilliant.'

'That sounds nice, but can I just ask, have you heard the term friends with benefits before?'

'No, but it fits us perfectly, doesn't it?'

'Well, that depends on whether we're sleeping together or not.' Rosie couldn't believe she'd actually said that out loud, but she had to know if he understood what he was saying.

'What do you mean?' he asked cautiously.

'Friends with benefits means friends who sleep together, but don't get involved in a relationship.' She almost asked if that was what he wanted with her, but was beginning to realise she was on the wrong track.

'Oh! I didn't know that,' he smirked.

'Right.' Rosie presumed that his smirk meant that he really did know what the phrase meant, but did that mean he was just teasing her, or did he really want them to be friends with benefits? She didn't want to know the answer because she wouldn't be happy to be considered a fool, but she also didn't want to agree to an affair when she cared for him so much. 'I'm going in the sea again,' she said as she quickly jumped up and hurried away.

Theo sat staring after her in confusion. He thought they were having a laugh, but she seemed to be offended that he was teasing her. It was only a silly little thing, but obviously he needed to apologise and make things right between them again. He didn't want to lose her as a friend and he certainly hadn't been trying for *those* kinds of benefits.

He gave her a little time to enjoy her swim and then decided to join her and put things right.

'You're a great swimmer, your body just flows through the water like a dolphin,' he said supportively. Make her feel good about herself and then move in for the apology.

'Thanks. I'm enjoying my swim today and feeling the rhythm of the waves.' Rosie was thrilled with the compliment and encouraged by the fact that he was coming so close to where she was almost chest-high in the water.

'I just need to be clear about what I was suggesting earlier, so we can hopefully move forward together without any awkwardness,' he began as he approached.

Rosie felt shivers run up her spine; hearing that Theo was explaining that he really wanted to be with her, even on a casual basis, was more than she could have hoped for. She didn't want to spoil his relationship with Selina and she'd hoped to fall in love with someone who was single, but this was the way it was and there was no way she could refuse.

'I completely understand and I'm totally on board with it,' she replied, as she moved to be nearer to him.

Suddenly, a rogue wave swept them together as though fate had taken a hand and Theo put his hands around her bare midriff to stop her from falling over.

In a moment she was kissing him and realising that she had no control whatsoever over her emotions. Whatever he wanted, she would give and if things got complicated, she would have to live with the consequences, but for now she was in heaven.

Theo and Selina were making their way to the harbour to board the sunset cruise which Leandra had suggested as a double date with her and the latest temporary crush.

'Why are we doing this again?' Theo asked with a sigh.

'Because she got some cheap tickets and she wants to have a romantic date.'

'It's hardly going to be romantic for her, with her sister in tow. You'd think she'd rather be alone with him somewhere.'

'But that's how it's been so far. They've just been hooking up and going to his place. She wants to enjoy a romantic date with him to see if they've got more than just a physical connection.'

'They could have just gone to dinner in Zia; that's what everybody else does.'

'I know, but this is what she wants so we're supporting her.'

'It's a bit of a tourist trap though, isn't it? A sunset cruise? What's the point?'

'I know, it's not really my kind of fun either, but a lot of people like it, so it might be worth a try,' Selina suggested half-heartedly.

'As long as you don't expect any romance from me,' he laughed.

'When do I ever? Everyone knows we're not the romantic type. I mean, watching the sunset is nice enough, but it's not as good as the sunrise and anyway I'd prefer to watch it while I swim in the sea rather than floating above it.'

'Hmm,' he nodded, thinking about the last time he had been in the sea.

'Look, we just need to do this for Leandra and then hopefully things will go well with this new guy and she'll be off with him all the time instead of bugging us to keep her company.'

'Right. Does he have a name? This new guy?'

'Of course he does, I just don't know it yet.'

'Does she know it?' he asked with raised eyebrows.

'Don't start. And try to be polite when you meet him instead of picking him to pieces.'

'It's more fun if I play the bad guy.'

'But he won't know you're just teasing. Not everyone likes it.'

'I know,' he replied, realising how teasing could sometimes be taken the wrong way.

'So just keep it to a bit of small talk and we'll be fine.'

'Are we fine?' he asked suddenly.

'What do you mean?'

'I mean, we don't enjoy things like this sunset cruise, we're happy to leave the romantic stuff to other people and we have completely different hobbies. It's nights like this that make me wonder if we're missing out somehow?'

'I don't think so. We give each other space to do the things we love, we know each other well enough to understand what the other person needs and we respect each other to believe we'll always have the other's back.'

'You're right,' he smiled happily.

'If you need something more, just tell me what it is and we can bring it into our lives.'

'No, we have everything we need. I was just wondering if we should be doing more couple-inspired events like this date night so that we look normal to everyone else, but then I realised if we're happy just being together doing ordinary stuff, then we're already normal and everyone else can take a hike.'

'Exactly. Sometimes we're just sitting on your sofa, eating peanuts and drinking beer, and I don't want to be anywhere else. It's all I nccd.'

'Yeah, we make a good team. Who needs all that excitement and making an effort all the time? I'd prefer to be sitting on a quiet beach in my tatty shorts and covered in sea spray, rather than turning up here in a suit and tie.'

'And I'd rather be make-up free with my hair swirling in the wind as I gaze over the mountains at the thermal springs, rather than pretending to be something I'm not on this double date.'

'I love how we always feel the same about these things,' Theo announced as they made their way on board.

'Me too,' Selina agreed.

SEPTEMBER

The group on Rosie's tour had been particularly demanding that day and she was looking forward to a much-needed break when she delivered them to the market.

There had been so many questions and she simply couldn't answer them all. She had all the historical details for the places they visited, but she had no way of knowing if the storms in Athens would be heading towards the island, she didn't know the name of a particular bird which crossed their path, she couldn't say if there would be the same children's discount on holidays for next year and she definitely had no idea what was happening between her and Theo.

Obviously, the last question was not one that the holidaymakers would have asked, but it was the one at the forefront of her mind and she didn't seem to be able to think about anything else.

She'd heard nothing from him since that day at the beach and the way things had been left, she didn't think it was up to her to make the first move. She had made it very clear how she felt about him when she pressed herself against him and kissed him passionately, but after that embrace they had left the beach and he'd dropped her at the bus station in order to give him time to complete a forgotten errand.

She tried to remember that amazing kiss, but the details were lost in a haze of pleasure and desire. He had kissed her back, she was sure, but she couldn't remember what he'd been doing with his tongue or his hands. It was possible he hadn't used his tongue, but not everyone did, and she definitely knew he had caught her when that first wave swept them together, so he must have had his hands on her waist, at least.

It was infuriating to be unable to recall the finer details because she was sure it was the most sensual moment of her life. Then it hit her. A sensual moment. That's what it was, just a moment. It had felt like everything to her, to finally kiss the man she had been crushing on for months but in the end, it had only been a short moment. As soon as the next wave hit them, he had quickly moved away and said they needed to get back to shore as the current could be dangerous and knock them off their feet. She was flattered by his concern for her, expecting to continue their dalliance on the beach, but he reached for his phone and said he'd had a reminder about picking up something for his mother, which he had forgotten all about. That had brought a sudden end their moment and they had parted without discussing what happened next.

She knew it was a huge step for him and that he must be so confused about his feelings, both for her and for Selina. She couldn't push him to talk about it and she definitely didn't want to scare him off by demanding some kind of clarification, but she had expected at least a casual text asking how she was. The connection between them was undeniable, but she could only presume it had been a huge surprise to him to finally act on it and she was prepared to give him time to come to terms with it.

She tried to believe in the phrase that no news is good news, but in the back of her mind she couldn't help thinking that he was in such a committed relationship already, that he might just not be able to see the potential they had to be happy together.

She hoped that they would have the chance to be alone on their break so that they could discuss their feelings and work out how things were going to move forward. If he said he couldn't be unfaithful to Selina, that would mean a choice between giving him time to break up with her before they went public with their own romance or, and she had to be realistic, losing him altogether. She knew which she would prefer, but it had to come from him.

The chances were that, if he broke her heart and stayed with Selina, she would have to go back to Ireland. Two emotional break-ups in under a year was not something she could recover from easily and she would need to surround herself with more security and familiarity. It felt like an ultimatum to say it was either a new start with Theo or I will have to go back home, but it was something she had to prepare herself for before they had the conversation.

She wasn't sure if she even wanted the conversation, but she couldn't handle the stress anymore and she kicked herself, again, for falling in love with a soon-to-be-married man, instead of one of the hundreds that were available all over the island.

As she entered the market place and began to show the group around, she saw Selina smile and give her a big wave, making her instantly nauseous. She really liked Selina and had originally promised herself that she would leave them alone to be happy together but since that kiss, she had realised that Theo felt the same for her, so she couldn't deny what they could build together. She wondered how they would be able to chat if all three of them took their break at the same time; it would be agony for her and Theo to hide their feelings, along with the guilt, but poor Selina would be totally unaware of what was going on. She hated that idea and quickly tried to work out how she could let Theo know to arrange something private.

She looked over to his stall as she pointed out to the group some wine bottles which had been produced from a distillery in the centre of the island, but couldn't catch his eye. She turned towards her customer as they asked exactly where the distillery was for future reference and when she looked back, she saw him disappear towards the staff area in the kitchen.

At first, she was a little confused as to why he would avoid her when she was almost ready to reveal the delights of his stall, but then presumed he wanted her to follow him to the kitchen, where they could speak more privately before an official break. It made her heart sing to know that he wanted to make time for her and she felt confident that she was special enough to him to expect some good news.

She mesmerised her group with tales of ancient battles and traditional customs as she described the secrets held by most of the ornaments on his stall, then advised her group that any items could be paid for at the main till in order to give Theo more time to talk.

She reminded them of the meeting time outside the museum and, after checking that Selina was busy with her own customers, quietly slipped through to the kitchen.

Theo was nowhere to be seen. She looked around the side corridor, but he was not there. She quickly popped her head out of the back door to see if he might be taking in a delivery, or having a breather, but the general goods area was empty.

She didn't know what to think and simply gazed in confusion at the table in front of her, where someone had left a list, or some notes. She moved over to look more closely and saw that it was a scrawled message saying that the person had gone to keep a dentist appointment and it was signed with the letter T.

She knew that stood for Theo and that he wouldn't have been able to put her name on the top, but really didn't understand why he didn't just quickly tell her he had to go, or send her a text, instead of presuming she would go looking and find the note. It was written in English, which assured her she was meant to see it, but also knew it was common in the market as there were lots of different nationalities working there. She was about to pick it up and put it in her pocket, to feel a little closer to him, but realised that there were other people who might need to know where he was. She brushed her fingers over the hurriedly scribbled words and then left it for others to find.

Rather than get stuck having to sit through her break making polite conversation with Selina, she skipped out of the back door and headed around the corner to the Old Town. She'd been there before, but didn't go regularly so it was nice to feel like a tourist for a change.

She wondered how it would feel if she came to live in the town and found herself walking this way on a daily basis. The bus station was just on the other side, so she would need to make the journey regularly if she was still meeting up with her regular tours around the island. She remembered Theo's comment about doing tours of his own and hoped he would still have her in mind to help out with that; it was something they could create and enjoy together. Many times, she would be in the middle of a tour and realise how much she was enjoying herself, considering where she would go and what she would say if it was her own business. Obviously, that would never happen without some financial backing and a lot of local support, but she knew it would be something she would be good at and would give her the job satisfaction she had never yet quite achieved.

She stopped for a moment outside a shop which was selling lots of wooden items. There were chess boards, salad servers, picture frames, egg cups and many more delightful keepsakes, but the one which caught her eye was a statue of a hunky Greek man with an unsurprisingly huge appendage. She giggled, remembering that first conversation with Theo and how he was now known by that term on her phone. She wanted to buy it as a reminder, then she wanted to take a picture of it and send it to him with a jokey comment, but she did neither as that was what friends, or lovers, would do. At that moment, she didn't know which one she was and, with his recent disappearing acts, she didn't know if she would ever be either of them. Her head told her that she had to face him and find out what that kiss meant to him and if he wanted to explore where it might lead, but her heart said she wasn't ready for the rejection and couldn't bear to know if he didn't want to be with her, so she decided to ignore the temporary lack of communication and continue to live in hope for a little while longer.

As Theo was nowhere to be found, Selina asked Panos to join her on their break.

The square was busy with an event organised by the local school and there were children everywhere, so they each decided to grab a takeaway coffee and enjoy a stroll along the harbour for a change.

'It looks completely different without all the boats docked here,' Panos said as he realised that he only passed the harbour before and after work, when all the boats were lined up and ready for customers.

'Yes, it's a completely different atmosphere when they've all gone out for the day. It reminds me of the winter, when they're all moored somewhere else.'

'Except that it's about fifteen degrees warmer today,' he said, loosening his collar a little.

'That's true, but it does make the harbour look more local, and less touristy, when it's not crowded with the boats and all their advertising.'

'I guess so, but without that tourism, the islands would suffer; they all depend on it now.'

'I know and I appreciate it in the summertime, but I do love the winters when it's just the locals; I feel more myself then.'

'I think we all do really. Greece has two distinct personalities when it's all hustle and bustle in the summer heat, then natural and traditional in the winter when everything slows down and there's time to communicate and enjoy life.'

'It's fun in a way, because if things were the same all year round, I wouldn't be able to appreciate each season separately and make the most of what it offers. Then again, there are some summers I wish it was winter instead and then some cold winters when I wish it was summer already,' she laughed.

'I've been there,' he smiled. 'Last winter, when we had all that snowfall up in the north, I remember wondering how my street could be so cold and icy when it could also be a scorching thirty-five degrees only six months later. It was a shock to the system.'

'Nature is full of surprises,' she agreed. 'I know it can be challenging sometimes when it reaches the extremes of temperatures, but if it was the same every day, what would we talk about?'

They both nodded in amused reflection.

'Have you had any thoughts about what you might do this winter?' he asked cautiously.

'Same as usual, I expect,' she shrugged.

'Will you be volunteering for the olive picking again?'

'Ooh, yes. It's my favourite time of the year.'

'Do you always stay here, or have you tried anywhere else?'

'It's always been here; just easier to join in when it's on the doorstep.'

'I suppose so,' he pondered, 'but aren't you tempted to see what happens somewhere else? There might be different methods of production in a larger operation and, at the same time, it would be a chance to meet some different people.'

'I'm not sure how I'd explain that to my parents. They like the routine.'

'But sometimes you have to think about yourself, and what would make you happy.'

'Like you do with the painting?'

'Yes, I made a choice and once everyone could see how determined I was, they let me give it a try. I can't say they're all totally behind me yet, but they knew it was important enough to explore the possibilities.'

'But you're brilliant! How could they not be behind you? They should be proud of how talented you are.'

'Hopefully they will be proud when they hear about my new offer, but I have you to thank for that.'

'Oh? Is it connected to the piece we did together? I'm still blown away by how beautiful that was and I've got the photograph of it pinned to my mirror at home.'

'The customer absolutely loved it and has asked for three more so that he can display them together.'

'That's wonderful! But, do you mean he wants me in the new paintings too?'

'Yes, so I have to check if that's alright with you first, but I can use the photographs we took that day and just change some of the colours and shading.'

'But that would be boring, if I'm just in the same kind of pose, surely?'

'And this is the tricky bit. He's happy to have a similar feel with the other paintings, with a woman looking out over the landscape, but he's enquired if there's any chance of something more.'

'More? Oh, you mean...' she gulped with embarrassment.

'I'm not sure what you're thinking, but it's nothing seedy. You can still be wearing the same kind of outfit and you could continue to look away from the viewer, so no change there.'

'So what's the "more" that this person is asking for?' Selina was surprised to have the opportunity to work with Panos again, but she knew straight away that she wanted to do it, especially when she knew she could stay covered up.

'He has made a few suggestions and he's waiting for my feedback before we make any arrangements.

As I said, he is more than happy to have similar paintings to the one he already has if I can find other suitable positions around the island which can evoke the same kind of feeling, but he wonders if I can create something a bit more personal, for at least one of them.'

'I'm still not sure what you mean?'

'He is interested in the face behind, what he calls, the mysterious lady, and is hoping that he could see more of your features next time. I told him you had modelled for me under the agreement that your face wasn't seen, and he is happy to continue without, but begged me to ask if you would consider at least a partial reveal of a cheekbone, or shadowed profile.'

That was as much as Panos could describe without revealing the real words his client had used, because it would be difficult to say that he had picked up on the obvious adoration of the artist for the subject and had ignited a curiosity which was itching to be satisfied.

'Oh, well, I suppose that wouldn't be too bad,' she replied as she considered the offer.

'There is a little more. He told me that if you were prepared to reveal part of your face, he would ideally like the setting to be at a window, where you are relaxing on a sofa, or day bed, and gazing out at the view of the sea as though you were awaiting someone's return.'

'That's quite specific,' she observed.

'I know. He has no expectations and he's willing to pay well for two or three more paintings similar to the one he has, but he is prepared to pay a whole lot more for one bespoke piece.'

'How much more?' she asked with selfish interest.

'Three times more. And you know how much he paid for the last one.'

'No way! That's unbelievable,' she gasped. 'But, of course, totally worth it for one of your paintings.'

'That was a good save,' he smiled. 'I said I would talk it over with you and let him know either way.'

'Well phone him up and tell him yes; you can't miss this opportunity.'

'I think we need to discuss the options first and whether we both want to do this.'

'Of course, we'll have to work out *how* we can do it, but why wouldn't we *want* to do it?'

'I didn't think you wanted to show your face and, even if you didn't mind that, you would be the main focus of the painting so it would take more than just one sitting to complete.'

'I was only glad you weren't showing my face before because I was too lazy to put any make up on!' she admitted. 'I don't want to have to use as much as a catwalk model, but I'd be happy to use enough to highlight my features. Also, if I'm looking out of a window, I won't be face-on anyway, so it won't be a big deal.'

'If you're sure, I would really appreciate it. Obviously, I'll pay you for your time.'

'Don't be daft, I'll enjoy doing it. Who else can say they've been headhunted to be the focal object of a painting by a bestselling artist?'

'Not sure I'd go that far, but if you're on board I could start to search for a few places we might be able to use, then you can check out which you like best.'

'I'm not the artistic one, so I'll leave that up to you. Just let me know when you've found the ideal spot and I'll be there.'

She didn't have to wait long.

A week later, Panos had found a luxury apartment on Airbnb which overlooked the shipping lane towards the sponge diver's island of Kalymnos. He had checked with his client and agreed that having a ship in the distance would create the perfect atmosphere for the piece and he could see the whole thing in his mind's eye immediately.

He arranged to co-ordinate shifts with Selina and rented the room for the three days he expected he would need.

On the first day, he arrived an hour before Selina to set everything up and make sure they had enough drinks and snacks. They only had three hours to confirm the positioning and get the basic shapes and sizes sketched out, then they would have a full day on the Sunday to take their time and create some magic. The final day would again be just a few hours to iron out any imperfections.

Selina was happy with the arrangement and loved how Panos had set up the scene. He'd moved one of the beds in front of the patio doors, which had a retro wooden finish, and it did look as though she would be gazing out of a window when the scene was pictured from waist-height.

She had brought many different items of clothing in several muted colours and she had fun running in and out of the bathroom trying each one individually and debating its benefits with Panos. She wrapped her hair in a chignon and allowed a few tendrils to loosen and caress her cheek, before moving to the bed and trying various positions until they found something which looked appropriate, while being comfortable enough to hold for lengthy periods at a time.

He noted all the relevant marker points and took several photographs of Selina so that they could accurately reproduce her posture and hair design. He took a couple of extra shots when one of her dress straps fell down, leaving her neck completely bare. How he wished he could paint the scene which that evoked in his mind.

Once the initial details had been finalised and the early sketches were complete, they left the scene ready to continue the next day.

This time Selina arrived first and gave herself enough time to apply a little make up, dress in the chosen outfit and arrange her hair as close to the design they had agreed as she could manage without the photograph which was on Panos' phone.

She moved over to the window scene and looked out to sea, avoiding the rumpled sheets on the bed so that she didn't disturb the specific look he had created. She tried to imagine how it would feel if she really was waiting for someone that she loved to return to her. She would no doubt be excited and eager to see that ship appear on the horizon, but what if they had been away for a long time? Might they have changed their mind? Maybe they didn't love her anymore? What if she was waiting for someone who was only returning to tell her that they now loved someone else?

What if she was the one who no longer was in love? What if she had to wait for a returning lover, who had been abroad, maybe fighting in a war, only to confess that she had fallen head-over-heels for someone she had just met? What if she still loved the returning soldier, but was no longer in love with him because she had recently found someone who made her feel alive with hope and desire. What if he had made such an effort to return to her and she had to break his heart so that she could become the person she was supposed to be, with another man?

'Oh, you're here already,' Panos said as he entered the room. 'Selina, what's wrong?' he asked as he rushed over to her and put his arm around her shoulders, wiping away the tear that was falling and threatening to ruin her perfectly applied mascara.

'Nothing, really,' she sniffed and dabbed at her eyes with a tissue. 'I don't really know where that came from, I was just getting into the mood for the painting and I got a bit emotional.'

'Are you sure? We don't have to do this if you're not totally happy with the arrangements.'

'No, I'm happy, really. I was just trying to imagine how it would feel to be waiting for something that could be life-changing and I got a bit carried away. Give me a few minutes and I'll be all set,' she said as she hurried to the bathroom to reset her thoughts.

Panos was concerned about Selina, but she seemed to return full of excitement and determination to do whatever it took to create the required atmosphere.

They settled into the same routine they had used on their previous session and the painting quickly began to take shape. They didn't speak quite as much as last time, because Panos was concentrating much harder and they didn't want to break the spell, so each of them became lost in their own world as the day unfolded.

Panos was a professional and was totally focused on creating the piece of art for which he had been commissioned. Apart from the moments he was focused on Selina. He had explained that sometimes when he was challenged with a specific item, he would just go into the bathroom for a few minutes to clear his mind and come back with a different perspective, so they had agreed it would be a quiet time while that process took place. However, he was finding that he needed to escape more often than usual because he was unbearably distracted by the sight of Selina lounging on a bed amongst ruffled sheets which appeared to have become misplaced through an intimate connection. That would have been enough to distract anyone, but the thought of being alone with her as she rolled around in the sheets was difficult enough, without having to paint that delicate and tempting neckline which he was so desperate to cover in kisses. He hoped he could complete the painting without losing his mind, but wasn't sure he would be able to let it go if he did.

Meanwhile, Selina was lost in her dreams of waiting to meet up with the returning soldier. She hadn't been able to let go of the feeling that she had to put an end to a misplaced relationship in order to be happy with someone who wanted her to live her best life. She couldn't really understand where that feeling was coming from and couldn't shake the emotion it produced as she sat there trying to pose calmly for Panos. She tried to imagine that the soldier was Kyriakos, who she cared for deeply, and that she was ending things with him to be with Theo, but something wasn't working and that was making her even more emotional. Each time Panos went into the bathroom to refocus his concentration, she closed her eyes and took a deep breath to steady the nerves which kept arising as she considered her dream scenario, but they remained. She knew that she shouldn't feel nervous to end something with the wrong person, to be with the right person, but every time she pictured giving up her life to be with Theo, there was no escape. It really didn't make any sense to her, but it was a fact and her emotions were all over the place.

Towards the end of the day, Panos relaxed into a chair, although his jaw was tense and tired. He was glad with what he had done and knew the finishing touches would be easy enough to complete the following day.

Selina sat back on the bed, resting against the headboard and taking in the changing colour of the sky as the sun began a slow decent over the sea.

'Come and watch this, it's beautiful,' she suggested.

He stiffly raised himself from the chair and sank into the softness of the mattress like it was some kind of cocoon.

'Oh, that's better,' he murmured as he perched at the edge.

'Come up here, there's a perfect view from this spot.'

He did as she asked, too tired both mentally and physically to resist. She was right.

They half lay in the fading sunlight as the rose-tinted sky grew into a fierce glowing red, then gradually evaporated into a pale grey, then dark grey, then black.

Both of them slept soundly in each other's arms for an hour or so, until Panos was disturbed by a beep from one of their phones. He awoke to find the woman of his dreams cuddled up against him in the same bed he had imagined rolling around on with her. She moved slightly and he realised that his face was resting on her shoulder and his lips were only millimetres away from her neck. He couldn't help himself and pressed them lightly onto her skin. It was as perfect as he had imagined.

He wanted so much to kiss her properly and tell her that she deserved so much more from her life than what she was currently settling for, but he was unselfish enough to know that it would have to be her decision and it wasn't his place to force that situation. She looked so beautiful lying there peacefully and he allowed himself to pretend, just for a moment, that they really were a couple and were lying in each other's arms after making love for the first time. He was in heaven. He knew he should wake her so that they could both go home, but he was sorely tempted to let her sleep, next to him, in a bed that was already paid for until tomorrow.

Her phone beeped again and she stirred very slightly. If she was waking up, he only had one more moment, so he leaned in and kissed her neck again, but in desperation it was deeper than before and she reached for him as she woke.

He pretended to be just waking up himself, but was thrown when she moaned softly and tilted her face up to kiss him on the lips. He wanted it to be real, but knew she was still half-asleep and not aware of what she was doing, so he gently held her shoulders and eased her back.

'Selina, hey, wake up,' he muttered softly.

'Mmm. I'm awake,' she mumbled.

'We fell asleep and I think someone's trying to message you.'

'It's OK,' she drawled and cuddled up to him even tighter.

'No, I think we need to make a move.' Panos couldn't believe how he had Selina pushing up against him, wanting him to hold her, and was moving away from her to send her home.

'I don't want to move,' she said as she leaned forward and began to kiss him again.

'Selina! Wake up!' he shouted out of desperation. One more second and he would be kissing her right back.

'What?' she groaned impatiently, leaning back and slowly opening her eyes. 'Oh, Panos!'

'Yes, we fell asleep,' he repeated as he jumped off the bed and reached for her phone. 'Someone's trying to contact you.'

'Oh, it's not... I can't...' She grabbed the phone and ran into the bathroom.

While she was in there, he tried to make sense of what had just happened. She had been asleep, so she must have thought he was Theo. That was the only explanation. Wasn't it? Should he ask her? Would he ever taste those amazing lips of hers again?

'Sorry, I have to go,' she called over her shoulder as she ran out of the bathroom, grabbed her bag and disappeared straight out of the door.

At the end of the month, Kyriakos celebrated his name day and invited a few of the workers to join him at his parents' house, where they had organised a small party for him.

There was a lot of talking, quite a bit of traditional music and a little spontaneous dancing, but Theo didn't think it was really what Kyriakos would have had in mind for himself on such a special celebration.

'I thought you'd be downing the cocktails at one of the nightclubs by now.'

'Yeah, so did I, but you can't avoid a family get together when it's made clear what an effort they've made for you. And it's actually quite nice to spend some down time with my nearest and dearest,' Kyriakos smiled, as he watched his grandmother telling her daughter-in-law that she had ruined some of the sweet pastries.

'But you'll still be going to the club after this?'

'Hell yeah!'

'How come Vitaly isn't here?' Theo asked casually. He was sure they were a couple and with everything out in the open now, it seemed strange that he wouldn't be there for such a special occasion.

'Let's go in the garden,' Kyriakos replied, before leading him past several relatives, around the terracotta pots and into the small shed around the back.

'So… either you have something secret to tell me, or this is your way of letting me know you fancy me?' Theo said lightly.

'No one knows about Vitaly,' Kyriakos gulped.

'Well of course we do. You two can't be apart for more than five minutes without some kind of excuse to "help" each other with a delivery or a display.'

'No, I mean, none of my family know about him.'

'Because…'

'Because it's taking them some time to come to terms with my news. They refused to believe me at first, but then other friends and relatives showed their support and they started to drop any talk of girlfriends or grandchildren.'

'Well, that's a start,' Theo muttered with more than a little sarcasm.

'They're just old-fashioned and they haven't had to deal with knowing anyone like me before.'

'You mean they've never met an openly gay person before.'

'No,' he replied quickly, checking that no one was hovering outside the door.

'You can say the word, you know. You're gay and that's fine.'

'It's not fine yet. I thought they'd accepted it and I was giving them some time to get used to it before Vitaly and I officially come out as a couple, but…' he shrugged without further explanation.

'There's no but. If you want to be with Vitaly, you shouldn't have to hide it. It's not good to feel so much for someone and not be able to express it.' Theo shocked himself at the power, and hidden meaning, of his words.

'But yesterday I overheard my mum talking to my aunt as they were organising things for tonight, and she said that she thinks it's a phase and she's sure I'll come to my senses when I meet the right woman.'

'Ah. So she hasn't really accepted it then?'

'She can't have if she's just biding her time until I grow out of it, or whatever. I was really hoping to share my happiness with my family tonight, but if they're not really behind me, how can I introduce them to Vitaly?'

'You could introduce him as a work mate and then, once they get to know how lovely he is, you can say you've grown closer and he's now your partner. They'll already love him, everybody does, so it will be much easier.'

'Yes, that's probably a good idea, but I can't bear to wait for months and months until they get used to seeing him around, plus how on earth do I keep my love for him hidden when we're in front of them? It's just such a big mess.'

'It really isn't. Look, clearly you love each other and want to be seen as a couple, yes?'

'Well, in an ideal world, yes.'

'But you only think your family will to refuse to accept the situation because they don't truly understand how you're feeling, so you need to take some time and explain to them again about what you want from life and how you've found someone who can give that to you.'

'It's so hard.'

'If it was a woman that you were telling them about, would it be that hard?'

'No, obviously.'

'There's no obviously about it. You are sure of your feelings and what you want from your life and whether that's due to a woman, a man, a dog or a dream job, it shouldn't matter. The fact is you've found what you want and need, so that should be enough.'

'On paper, I agree with you, but this is my parents we're talking about. They still live in the 20th century, or maybe the 19th, and these things didn't happen in their day.'

'Oh, of course they did. Gay men have been around for ever! As much as all this seems to be new to you, you're not actually the first man to discover he's gay.'

Kyriakos made another quick check to confirm that no one was standing outside to overhear their conversation.

'Why do you keep checking if someone is there? They all know you're gay, you told me that many of them were supportive.'

'Yes, they were, but since the announcement nothing more has been said. It seems like it's OK for me to be…'

'Gay,' Theo announced firmly.

'Gay,' Kyriakos agreed more timidly. 'As long as I don't make them uncomfortable by talking about it or being open about my desires'.

'And how long do you think you'll be able to keep that up? If you're still hiding the truth and denying yourself the kind of life you deserve, you've no more come out than I have.'

'Can you help me? How can I make them understand that I just want them to be happy for me, now that I've found someone wonderful to love?'

'I'll do my best,' Theo responded, suddenly recognising how his friend's situation was echoing some of the difficulties he was currently having, but he didn't want to think about that while Kyriakos needed his help. 'Why don't you give Vitaly a call and ask him to meet us here, before we leave for the club? That way, he can say a quick hello so everyone will remember him, but he won't be around long enough for you to feel awkward about hiding your feelings in front of him. Then, when we leave you can be a normal couple again. From now on, we'll make sure he is included more often and get some of your supportive family members to make him feel welcome. We'll make this work, I promise.'

'Thank you, so much. I really don't want to lose him because my family won't accept something they don't fully understand.'

'It's obvious you belong together. If you know you can make it work, it shouldn't matter how many challenges you face to get there.'

'You're right. I think when you meet someone who really understands you, and enjoys the same things as you, and loves all your funny little ways... and all of your not-so-funny little ways, you will do whatever it takes to have them in your life. I don't think I really knew what true love meant before, but I do now,' Kyriakos said with a contented smile.

'I know what you mean. It's that feeling when you know what they're going to say before they say it and you know they'll support whatever crazy ideas you come up with.'

'Yes, that's it. They just accept you for who you are and don't try to change you in any way. It's even better when they know just how to surprise you with something special that you don't even remember telling them you liked.'

'Yeah, I'm not really keen on surprises, but when it's something you like, it really shows that they understand where you're coming from.'

'Do you know, sometimes I think I can tell what is going through Vitaly's mind just by looking at him. He might be rubbing his nose, or pushing his hair behind his ear and I'll ask him about something specific and he'll say that was exactly what he was just thinking about.'

'I think that happens when you're really in tune with someone. I'll sometimes see the glint in those blue eyes and know exactly what is going on inside her head.'

'Brown eyes.'

'What?'

'Brown eyes. Unless I'm colourblind, Selina has brown eyes.'

'Oh, yes. That's what I meant,' Theo nodded.

'Well, thank you for the chat and the help. You've made me more determined to sort this out and live the life I'm supposed to have, rather than the one they think I should settle for.'

'You're welcome. You deserve the best,' he confirmed as they leaned in for a man-hug, exactly as the shed door was swiftly pulled open.

'What exactly is going on here then?' a stern voice asked.

'Oh no, this isn't…' Kyriakos began, as laughter greeted him from the other side of the door.

'Your face!' Selina whooped as she wobbled on the uneven pathway. 'Your mum was wondering where you were so I came to look, but it's a good job it was me who found you and not her.'

'Yes, that would have been hard to explain,' Kyriakos grimaced. 'But then again, how do you know nothing was going on? Maybe I've tempted your lover to the other side.'

'As if! We're joined at the hip, aren't we babe?' she said in a decidedly tipsy version of celeb-speak. 'Come on, we've got to find some sherry for your aunt… erm… I've forgotten her name,' she giggled.

'I'll come and sort it out,' Kyriakos said, as he accompanied her back to the house to make sure she arrived safely. She wasn't one to get drunk very often.

Theo sat and mulled over some of things he'd revealed in their conversation.

'It's not good to feel so much for someone and not be able to express it.'

'Take some time to explain what you want from life and how you've found someone who can give that to you.'

'If you're still hiding the truth and denying yourself the kind of life you deserve, you've no more come out than I have.'

He was sure he was just offering support to his friend and saying the things he needed to hear so that he could face his family and live the way he was supposed to. He was being supportive and thinking through how important it was to be honest and tell his nearest and dearest what he really wanted from life; that was the only way Kyriakos could find happiness.

But why were those words so etched in his own mind? Why was owning up and "coming out" about what was really important in life, such a vital step. Why did he feel that he was experiencing something similar in his own life and that there was a bright and happy future lying in wait for him if he just had the strength to face it and bring it out into the open?

Was it simply the fact that he had started to think more and more about a change of career? It would be a big change if he moved into guiding full time, rather than the occasional trip he had originally envisaged. Talking to Rosie had made him see that he might be happier following his dream and fulfilling his potential as a fully-fledged tour guide, showing visitors around and explaining the historical significance of all the artefacts there were to discover. It made him smile just to think of it and he was sure he would be happy following that path, but it would be so hard to explain to Selina and the rest of his family that he was giving up on the only thing he had ever known, for something that he couldn't even guarantee would work.

He convinced himself that it was worth the effort, but knew there would be challenges ahead. He just had to keep his mind focused and not allow those blue eyes to distract him again.

OCTOBER

As Panos was removing some of the stands from the flower stall, ready to go into storage, he caught sight of Leandra entering the market and quickly made a hasty getaway to the delivery bay. He hoped that in the time it would take him to load up the car with all the bits and pieces he had cleared so far, she would have got bored and moved on, as he was struggling to make her understand that he really wasn't interested in getting together with her.

He knew it was partly his fault, well, mostly his fault, but he had apologised for giving her the wrong idea and thought that should be enough. He was also afraid that she had spoken to Selina, which was more than he'd been able to do, and he couldn't imagine the tale she would have woven about what had happened between them. He decided that once Leandra had disappeared again, he would make time to speak to Selina and explain everything. Well, possibly not everything.

After the misunderstanding of the sleepy kiss, Panos had spent the night in the same bed, imagining how it would feel to receive that caress for real. He was unable to leave and was just counting down the hours until she returned the next day. He wondered if she had rushed away due to the phone message, or just because she was embarrassed over her misunderstanding and he worried for her either way. He presumed that she would have let him know if something awful had happened and therefore hoped that if she was just embarrassed, he could quickly reassure her that it meant nothing and they could just move on. He'd been lying about his feelings ever since he met her, so one more wouldn't matter, especially if it got them back to the easy way they usually were together.

The next day he'd replicated the scene with the use of the stock photos and only hovered over those of Selina for a few minutes. Well, maybe twenty, or thirty minutes, but it was only to ensure that he knew where he needed to make the final touches, even if none of them were to be the touch of his fingers on her face.

He sent her a light message saying how he was looking forward to completing the assignment, reminding her of the time and asking if she could possibly bring some bread and a couple of sweet treats from the bakery on her way. He hoped it sounded casual and dismissive, almost as though their moment of connection hadn't happened, but he knew it was something he would never forget.

He set up the canvas and mixed a few colours together, but he knew there really wasn't much left to do, he was actually just playing the game so that he could spend another couple of precious hours with Selina.

Time was moving on and he wondered if she had decided just to avoid him altogether, so he jumped when there was finally a knock on the door and he raced to answer it in a heightened state of excitement.

'Hi,' she said, somewhat nervously.

'Great to see you, come in,' he replied as casually as he could manage. She looked as gorgeously natural as ever, though appeared a little different and was being very cautious, but he wasn't surprised. She'd probably been unsure how to start things, so he decided to take the lead. 'I'm glad you decided to come. Why don't we just start again and forget that little misunderstanding yesterday?'

'Er… if you think that's for the best?'

'Definitely. I really like how things are between us and I'd hate for anything to change that.'

'Mmm. Me too,' she nodded, with a hint of curiosity.

'Well…' He had thought she might try to make excuses, or apologise, or maybe even say that she had intended to kiss him, but instead she was being very reticent which wasn't like her. He would have preferred to talk about it and get it out of the way, but if she simply wanted to dismiss it, that was probably for the best.

'Well? Where do you want me?'

It was a simple request, but again, out of character, because she knew exactly where she needed to be and they had formed a familiar way of working which needed very little query.

'Just in the same place as yesterday, but you can change and do your make up first; I've left the bathroom free for you to prepare.'

'Oh, yes, of course,' she smiled, holding his eyes for a moment before she continued on her way.

He took a breath and ensured that the bed was in the correct position, with the sheets as close to the photograph images as possible. Selina seemed really different, but he couldn't put his finger on exactly why. She hadn't said that the kiss was a mistake, or that she wished it hadn't happened, but she hadn't said that she'd wanted it either. He didn't know what to make of it, but as long as she didn't want to talk about it, he couldn't force the issue and would just let her show him how she wanted to deal with it.

She returned from the bathroom with slightly more make up than usual and her hair wasn't quite the same as yesterday, but he would enjoy the opportunity to tease it into place. She was also wearing one of the provided bath robes, which suggested a much sexier appearance than he required, but he was enjoying it all the same.

'So, if you sit on the bed, I'll arrange it so that it fits with what we did yesterday,' he said, as he lay a few photos out on the table for comparison.

'Well, this all looks very… cosy,' she smirked.

'I hope so; that's what we're aiming for. Yes, just sit there and see, your leg was slightly more forward,' he indicated as she moved into place. 'I should probably just tuck some of these loose pieces away,' he said, his heart beginning to race as his fingers brushed her silky hair.

'You've got the perfect touch,' she said huskily, as she turned her face towards him and he could feel the heat between them.

'I should be used to it by now,' he replied, swallowing an urge to move a couple of inches closer and taste those lips once more. Even though they inexplicably had an excessive amount of lipstick today.

'I don't mind if you want to practise a bit more,' she murmured suggestively, as she let the robe slip from her shoulders to reveal that exquisite neckline.

'Oh,' he involuntarily groaned in response, unable to hide his desire. He wasn't sure what the rules were, but she was obviously opening up to him and he was happy to enjoy whatever she was offering.

'I thought you might like that,' she said, as she leaned over and kissed him on the cheek, breathing heavily into his ear.

'As long as you like it too,' he said, moving to kiss her neck and hoping that much more would follow.

'Don't I always?' she asked strangely. 'I'd like it more if you did this,' she told him as she took his hand and wrapped it around her breast.

'Mmm,' he moaned. Words could not express the happiness he was feeling as he caressed the smoothness of her warm skin under his fingers, suddenly realising that she was completely naked under the robe.

'That's it, baby,' she said as she squeezed his hand harder and pulled him in for a kiss.

For the first few seconds, he was delirious. The most perfect woman in the world had let it be known that she was his, at least in that moment. He kissed her passionately and tried to ignore the unpleasant stickiness around her lips which was spreading itself all over his.

He realised that he didn't want his first encounter with Selina to be a rapid, passionate and steamy affair, especially if it turned out to be a one-off occasion; he wanted them to take their time and enjoy lots of romantic moments which he would be able to treasure forever. She was not the type to be unfaithful to a long-standing partner just to enjoy a quickie and then carry on as though nothing had happened, so he moved away from her face and began to gently kiss her neck, working down to where his hand was still caressing her womanliness.

'Ooh, yes, baby. That's it!' she cried out. 'And you can keep moving down if you want.'

'Mmm,' he moaned again, but less naturally. That just didn't sound like the Selina he knew and he would never have dreamed that she would come out with something so coarse. He was lucky enough to be living his dream, but it wasn't turning out to be quite the experience he had envisaged.

'Bite me!' she instructed.

The phrase sounded familiar, but he couldn't quite place it. He gave her skin a little nip.

'Come on tiger,' she said, in a voice he'd heard before, as she reached inside his shorts. 'I can't wait to feel you inside me again.'

What?

'Leandra?' he shouted as he pulled away from her and wiped his mouth with the back of his hand.

'Oh bugger, I was hoping you wouldn't realise it was me until I'd had my way with you,' she said with only a minimal amount of dissatisfaction.

'What the hell?' he said, infuriated, but unsure whether it was with her or with himself.

'Look, don't tell Selina, will you? I mean, she shouldn't be playing around with you anyway, but she'd kill me if she knew what I'd just done, even though she was the one who asked me to fill in for her.'

'What on earth?' He couldn't make sense of what she was saying.

'I'm sorry I pretended to be Selina, but to be honest I wasn't totally sure if my guess about the two of you getting it on was correct, so I was pleasantly surprised when I realised I could benefit from the situation. That was fun,' she smiled wickedly.

'You don't understand,' he said, trying to work out what was happening. Somehow, Leandra had suspected that something was going on between him and Selina, probably due to the secret way they had been meeting for the paintings. Now she had moved in, just as he was feeling particularly unsettled, making an awkward situation much worse. If he admitted that he had thought he was kissing Selina, that would cause all kinds of difficulties for them both and how would he explain that he had just gone along with it? But what other option did he have?

'Oh, I understand perfectly,' she said as she wrapped the robe around herself again. 'You and Selina are carrying on behind Theo's back and it's not right. She always gets what she wants and I just have to sit around watching. Well, not this time.'

'No, you really don't understand,' he shook his head and then tried to smile convincingly. 'Yes, I thought you were Selina when you first arrived, even though you did seem different, but by the time you came out of the bathroom, I knew it was you, Leandra. I've had a bit of a crush on you for a while, but it felt odd when I'm so friendly with Selina, even though you're worlds apart. When we started getting close I couldn't believe my luck, so I just played along with you to avoid spoiling the atmosphere and it was really nice. I was enjoying myself, but then you moved to take things a bit further and I realised that I would be leaving soon, so I couldn't just take advantage of you once and then leave, particularly if I hadn't even been able to use your real name.'

'What do you mean?' she asked in total surprise.

'I mean that I'm glad we've had that little moment together, really I am. But we can't take things any further because I'll be leaving soon and it isn't right.'

'Sure it is!' she beamed. 'We can have one mad, crazy, passionate night together and then say goodbye. It doesn't have to be difficult.'

'That's where we're different and why I haven't approached you before. I don't sleep around. When I share myself with someone it's because I love them and want to be with them every day. That can't happen with us, so I really can't start something that will end unhappily. I'm sorry.'

'Hmm. What if we just go back to rolling around on the bed and having a bit of fun?'

'I think the moment's passed. Also,' he added, while he had the chance, 'I agree that it's probably best if you don't mention this to Selina, like you said. I don't want to cause any friction between sisters and we've enjoyed working together up until now, so I don't really want to give her anything to be annoyed with me about.'

'Give me one more kiss before I go then, and I'll try to keep quiet,' she suggested with raised eyebrows.

He didn't really have a choice.

Since then, he had avoided her at every turn and Selina had simply apologised that she had been required elsewhere on that day and had to send Leandra in her place.

There had been a slight uneasiness between them but nothing had been mentioned, either about Selina's kiss, or Leandra's, and he was happy to forget the whole incident and move on. He had one more issue to discuss with Selina and it would be his final attempt to show her the kind of life she could have, even if he only played a minimal part.

As he returned to the stall, he could see that Leandra had gone and her sister was looking harassed.

'Do you need a coffee?' he asked. 'Looks like you've got something on your mind.'

If Leandra had spilled the beans about their encounter, he would have to speed up the removal process and leave tomorrow.

'Ugh! Leandra's just been in with some magazines that mum sent over.'

'That's not usually a problem?' he asked with relief.

'It is when they're wedding magazines.'

'Oh.'

'Exactly. They are really pushing me now. If they're trying to arrange all the details for the dress and the flowers and the church and... everything, right now, what are they going to be organising for the next three years? We really thought they'd back off once we gave them a vague idea of when it would be, but it's all systems go now and it's doing my head in,' she pouted as she sank low into her chair.

'Come on, you need a break,' he insisted, lifting her elbow and persuading her to join him in the staff rest room.

'Put a double shot of coffee in there, please,' she asked, as she massaged her temples.

'What can we talk about that will distract you?'

'Tell me your plans for the move back to Thessaloniki. Maybe I'll come to visit you during the winter. With Theo, obviously,' she added after a moment.

'Well, you'd be very welcome. In fact, I have some ideas which would make that a very good plan indeed.'

'Tell me more,' she asked with genuine interest.

'My agent has told me that she's organised a new exhibition for my work next February and she wants it to be along the lines of the paintings which have just recently sold so very well. And thank you again for that,' he smiled.

'It was really my pleasure,' she blushed.

'Obviously the landscapes can be found everywhere and additionally I can use the photographs we've taken, or even substitute a mannequin to replicate any human involvement, but if you were interested in doing a bit more modelling, I could pay you the going rate and you could help me out while you're visiting.'

'Oh! Surely you want a real model for that? I'm just...' she faltered.

'You were perfect. You did exactly as I asked and because you were enjoying yourself, it came across in the finished product. Sometimes the professional models are just bored and that is hard to disguise. I'd love it if you would think about it.'

'OK,' she smiled. 'I will.'

'There is something else that might tempt you.'

'Does it have anything to do with chocolate? Because that's something I wouldn't be able to resist right now,' she asked hopefully.

'No, but it might be something you like even more than chocolate.'

'At the moment, that would be hard to imagine.'

'It's olives, of course.'

'Of course,' she repeated. 'Why didn't I guess?'

'Well, depending on the timing, if you decide to come and help me with some more art work, there are several olive groves nearby which need help with the picking, so you would be able to enjoy your favourite hobby in a new place for a change.'

'That is, indeed, very tempting,' she nodded appreciatively.

'If you do decide to visit me, you could time it to begin with olive picking and then earn some more cash by doing a few sittings for me. I think you'd really enjoy it.'

'Sounds perfect.'

'I know.'

'I mean, it sounds perfect for me. I'd be busy having fun doing something I loved, but Theo would be just sitting around twiddling his thumbs with nothing to do.'

'He could do loads of sight-seeing. There are hundreds of places he could visit and he's said before how much he enjoys looking into the history of historical places of interest.'

'Yes, you're right, but it seems a bit odd to go somewhere together and then spend all our time apart. Usually, we just do the things we enjoy individually on our own, then meet up in-between for our regular arrangements.'

'Well then, what if you made several short visits on your own for a few days at a time to do the olive picking and then to sit for different paintings through the winter? That way, you'd get the best of both worlds.'

'Now that might be a plan,' she considered.

'It would certainly introduce you to the area and you'd also have a chance to find out about what's involved in the process of pressing the olives from a family business I know in Halkidiki. If you spent some time working there, you'd get a great hands-on experience and be able to decide if you want to take it further on your own.'

'Oh, no. That's never going to happen. It's just a silly dream.'

'No dreams are silly, Selina. I know you could do it; you just need more information about what's involved.'

'But I'm sure I couldn't afford to go it alone. It must cost a fortune to create a successful business.'

'Saying that just shows how you don't have enough information yet. Once you work out how much things cost and how much you can earn, you will see what kind of business you could develop. No doubt you would start small and build it up, but it would be something of your own, and something you really want to do.'

'And a lot of people want to win the lottery, but it's not as easy as that, is it?'

'No, but they have more chance if they at least give it a go.'

'I can't just leave the market and swan around the country learning a new craft while everyone else waits here and plans my wedding. It's ridiculous.'

'You're right. It is ridiculous.' He took a deep breath. It was now or never. 'If you would rather stay in the same place all your life, married to the only man you've ever really known, agreeing to whatever your parents think your wedding should consist of, and believing that you don't deserve to have the kind of life you really want, then go ahead. Stay here, let your wedding plans continue without any input from yourself, give up any chance of discovering what you're really capable of achieving and end any dreams of having a truly happy life.'

She glared at him in disbelief, but had no words to offer.

'I'm sorry to make it sound so awful, but it is. Settling for less than you are worth is terrible and I want to do whatever I can to help you avoid that. I stand by my offer for you to visit and enjoy some of the things that I know would make you happy. And I'll go one step further and then I'll stop.'

His brain was racing ahead, but he'd said too much to give up now.

'If you want, or need, to escape this treadmill you've found yourself on, and you're happy to discover where your passion truly lies, you can come and live in my studio in the garden without charge. You can earn money full time by sitting for me as a model, while learning all about the oil making process in the neighbouring village and I know, I truly believe, that you will be much happier than staying here and settling for less than you deserve. Think about it,' he said as he quickly abandoned her to ponder his words, because he had just emptied his soul and he had nothing left.

Theo was a little bored as he rearranged his display so that the items were more spread out and some of the decorative plates were in twos or threes rather than in piles of ten which generally saved space. At this time of year, he was just hoping to sell most of his remaining stock without having to reorder for the last few weeks as there was much less cash coming in and it was easier to replenish the stock in the spring, when there may also be new designs to choose from.

He took out his phone and scrolled through the last few messages he had exchanged with Rosie, knowing that it would be her last tour to the market today.

He hadn't been able to stop thinking about her, ever since that unexpected kiss in the sea. It had been slippery and salty and completely out of the blue, but he had enjoyed the sudden novelty of it, the feel of her skin under his fingertips and the temptation of her tongue in his mouth. It had only lasted for seconds, he wasn't sure how many, but it had been like nothing he had ever experienced before and it was on replay through his dreams every night. He couldn't understand why it felt so right when he knew it was wrong. So wrong.

He had avoided her to begin with, so that she didn't expect the same thing again, but then he realised it was his own fault for teasing her and giving her the wrong impression in the first place. He had to apologise, but didn't know how to do it without making her feel that it was all her misunderstanding, and as time passed it seemed easier to let it slide rather than bring it all back up again. That was when he had started to send her little messages about wanting to plan some small tours for the following year and asking bits of advice about anything he could think of. He also sent her a few GIFs and forwarded amusing posts so that they could still chat and laugh together without having to talk about what had happened. Whenever they took a break on market day, he made sure someone else was always with them, so that they didn't have to broach the subject and they could just ignore the silly mistake that it had been and carry on as friends.

He really wanted to be her friend and hoped they would be able to work together somehow the following year. He was still nursing the ambitious idea that they could form their own company and tailor the trip to suit them rather than the big tour companies, but he didn't want her to think there was more to it so he had put it off so far.

He also wondered how he could work with her in a professional way, when his dreams had been so vivid and enticing that he definitely was imagining her to be more than a friend on those occasions. He knew it was unkind to Selina to have those specific dreams, so he never told her about them, or the misunderstanding which had created them, but they had discussed similar dreams he'd had with Beyonce and Kylie and she hadn't worried about those. It had to be the same kind of thing, surely?

He sent Rosie a message, saying that he would take her to their favourite snack bar as a treat for her last visit. He added that it would be nice for them to have a chat on their own and discuss her options for the winter. He hoped that she had been able to save a little money by staying with her friend through the summer and would finally be ready to move to the town, where they could form some kind of plan for the next season.

As Rosie finished her introduction to the small amphitheatre on the outskirts of town and allowed her guests to wander around the grounds, she retrieved her phone from her bag, where she had heard it beep moments earlier. She smiled as she saw there was a message from her hunky Greek guy, but when she read its contents, she had to go and quietly sit on the coach to ponder over what it would mean.

She relished the idea of them being alone and not having to restrict the words they could say to each other, but she knew this was not going to be the romantic announcement she had hoped for. Theo had initially backed off after their kiss and had only contacted her after that in a vague, and definitely friends-only way. She had misread the whole situation down on the beach that day and he'd been teasing about the friends with benefits thing, she could see that now. The only thing she was still puzzled over, was why he kissed her back instead of pushing her off straightaway? She had finally remembered the details of his hands on her waist and the sensation of having his warm and wet body pressed up against hers and, even though it didn't last for long, the bliss of their lips meeting hungrily. It had been a very sexy and promising moment, quickly ended and apparently forgotten, by him at least. It was something that she would hold onto until she ever met anyone who could make her feel the same way again, but she didn't expect that would be any time soon.

She had a feeling that he would bring up the issue of living in town again and she just didn't know how to answer that. The idea of living so close to him and being able to see him more than just once a week made her happier than she'd been in a long time, but not being able to hold him, or tell him how she was really feeling would be simply unbearable. The fact that he was in a relationship with Selina somehow didn't make her jealous, they really were a lovely couple and clearly loved each other, but she just couldn't ignore her own attraction to him. It wasn't something she could just brush away and forget all about, so she would be constantly torn between wanting to see him and then having to endure sleepless nights when she had to head home alone. The problem was that she didn't want to stay on the island if she couldn't be near him and if she stayed with her friend over the winter, that would be what she would have to deal with. The only other option was to go back to Ireland, at least for the winter and weigh up whether she had anything to return for the following summer.

It was a hopeless situation and she didn't know where to turn for answers. She hadn't felt this confused over her recent break-up; she'd been let-down and her pride had been hurt, but she believed she had bounced back and was ready to move on. Unfortunately, the person she wanted to move on with was unavailable. No, that wasn't true. He wasn't interested, and there was a massive difference. As she thought over that realisation, she felt her heart thud as though part of it had just given up and fallen over. It was strange how she was having such physical reactions to thoughts of Theo; it hadn't happened with any other man in her life and she wasn't sure how to handle it.

She felt like some kind of naïve teenager who had fallen head over heels in love and wouldn't listen to any advice from friends and family. It felt as though it was the only thing in the world which mattered and nothing could dissuade her from that thought as she wrapped her arm around herself for comfort. She couldn't believe she hadn't realised what was happening over those summer months as she initially fancied Theo and then got to know the person underneath. She had thought she had loved before, but it was nothing like this. She really was in love! She wasn't sure she could keep it to herself now that she realised what was happening, because if ever there was proof that "the one" really did exist, for her it was Theo. If today was going to be the last time that they would meet, she couldn't leave without telling him how special he was.

She thought of nothing else until she reached the market and he hurried to meet her.

'I'll go and get our order in,' he said. 'Don't bother showing them around, there's no point when there are so few of them. Just show them where things are and then come and join me. Oh,' he added as an afterthought, 'if you also put your meeting time back by fifteen minutes, that should probably give us an extra half an hour.'

She wasn't sure which of them was smiling more, but it seemed they were both looking forward to some time together after all.

Theo and Selina left the gathering and headed straight for their favourite bar for a drink.

'Are they serious?' Selina fumed, as she downed half a glass of wine in one go.

'I think they are serious, but they're obviously off their heads,' Theo concurred, echoing her actions with his beer.

'How on earth can they say that now all the clothes and flowers have been decided, and the seating arrangements have been confirmed...'

'Which... I don't even know how they've got to that stage when we haven't seen any of it.'

'Exactly,' she nodded. 'How can they say we "might as well" bring the wedding forward?' Selina made a showy performance of creating quotation marks with her fingers, without spilling her drink.

'Because they'll never be satisfied, will they? I can't believe we got sucked into this when we made it perfectly clear we're happy to stay as we are for now.'

'You're right, it's all for them, isn't it? We're just pawns in their game and they're all planning the wedding that they want in a way, and at a time, which just suits them.'

'At this rate, we'd be just turning up to a wedding without having a clue who was coming, what food was being served, or who the bridesmaids and best man would be.' Theo put his glass down on the table rather forcefully, gaining a few side glances from nearby customers.

'But what if we just didn't turn up?' she asked with a sly expression. 'There can't be a wedding if we don't turn up, can there?'

'No, but we're not stupid enough to try that on; they'd probably frogmarch us down the aisle.'

'Yeah,' she shrugged. 'Plus, it really is going to cost a lot of money, so we couldn't let them waste it once they start paying the deposits.'

'We should just elope, that would be cheaper and a lot less fuss.'

'But they'll still have forced us to do it before we're ready, won't they?'

'Oh, yeah,' he shook his head. 'I need another drink.'

'Me too.'

Theo returned with a bottle of wine, knowing it would take more than just a few sips for them to calm down and make sense of the whole thing.

'Do you think they've even written our vows?' Selina asked sarcastically.

'I wouldn't be surprised. Mine will be promising to give you loads of healthy, happy children who look like mini versions of us.'

'And mine will be swearing to cook and clean and keep the house running perfectly until you return home in the evening.'

'For the record, I don't want a big family. Too many kids would drive me nuts.'

'And I want a real career before any of that happens, so you will probably be getting home before me anyway.'

'So, you're thinking of looking into the olive oil business?' he asked with interest.

'Well, I definitely am now. I need to give them a reason why it'll be impossible to bring the wedding forward. If I can find a farm, or even a faceless company, who'll give me a start, it would make perfect sense to delay the ceremony until I finish the training, at least.'

'Are there any farms here who are taking on staff full time?'

'I don't think so, they just want people to help with the picking for now because they're not big enough to do their own pressing and full production.'

'That's what I thought, from what you've said before. So, does this mean you're thinking of working away?'

'No, of course not. I can't leave the island. Or you,' she added automatically.

'But it would certainly throw a spanner in the works for the wedding preparations if you were somewhere else?'

'Well, obviously. Why? Do you think it's something you could live with?'

'I hadn't really thought about it but in this situation, I feel like telling you to go tomorrow!' he laughed, feeling the tension finally beginning to ease.

'And I definitely feel like taking off right this minute,' she said, with too much honesty.

'We should find out more about any availability there might be; after all, you have been saying for a long time that it would be a dream come true.'

'But would you really be OK with that? I mean, we could probably meet up from time to time, but we would be apart for most of the year.'

'What do *you* think? Could you cope without our pizza and beer nights?'

'I'm sure I would manage, as long as you could cope without our late-night swims at the thermal springs.'

'Ugh, how could I possibly live without that familiar smell of rotting eggs?' he laughed.

'Hmm, you might have a point there,' she shrugged.

'So, can you look into a place that might take on a few trainees? Who would know where to find a successful company?'

'Well,' she hadn't prepared for this situation, but it was too good an opportunity to miss. 'When I was casually talking to Panos about how much I love the whole olive thing, he mentioned a place up north that he knows covers all the basics. It sounded lovely, but I didn't get any details.'

'That's amazing! Get back in touch with him and find out where it is. There's no time to lose if you want to join in with this season's picking.'

'What? Right now? Don't we need to talk about the way we'll deal with being apart all the time?'

'Oh, er, I suppose so.'

They sat silently for a moment, imagining a scenario which neither of them had previously anticipated, even though their brains were racing ahead with how much they could achieve if they were to be free of expectations, for a while at least.

Selina was full of hope for the future, now that it seemed she might have the opportunity to follow her dream and get involved with olive oil production. It could be just the start she needed in order to discover if it would indeed be possible to create a business of her own in the future and have the independence to make her own decisions. She couldn't ignore the fact that Panos would be part of her life if she took the chance to begin again under his roof, and she allowed a fleeting image of his smiling face to confirm that it was something she really wanted.

Theo had only made the joke about Selina moving away to show how much he wanted to delay the wedding arrangements; he hadn't realised just how much she really wanted it and he knew it would make her happy. As long as she was happy, he was fine. It struck him, that he wanted her to be happy more than he worried about them being apart. They didn't live in each other's pockets anyway, so it was quite understandable that they would want to explore other career opportunities which might separate them for a while. He was also moving forward with his plans to create a new kind of tour around the places of interest in the town, with which Rosie had agreed to help him next year, if she decided to return from Ireland after her Christmas visit. She was still worried about the cost of renting a place on her own and he considered offering his spare room, but then she had confessed to being in love with him and he had frozen. He hadn't frozen with fear, or distaste, but with the fear of what he could do next, when he realised that he really liked knowing she felt that way. She had left him with that information, so that he could decide if he could still work with her, knowing how she felt. She had no other agenda, to come between him and Selina, but she had to be honest and he respected her for that. He almost loved her for it.

'Things will change between us, if I move away,' Selina began.

'Not that much. We'll be messaging and we can face time like we do now. Just instead of being down the road we'll be in another part of the country,' he observed simply.

'Yes, but our day to day will be different. We've been together forever and we're bound to feel it when we can't just tell each other what we had for lunch, or who's going out with who.'

'Maybe, but that's kind of all we do, isn't it?' he realised with a start. 'We should probably still be able to do that in a message.'

'Yes, I suppose we can. But we won't be able to spend quality time together...'

They both paused for long enough to realise that they couldn't remember the last time they had spent any quality time together.

'We might have to move to a different level of communication, but we can still keep each other involved in what's going on in our lives,' he suggested.

'Can we? Will it be enough?' she asked with concern.

'If we agree to make the effort. I'm sure we'll miss each other like crazy, but as long as we start and end the day with a good morning and a good night, I'm sure we'll survive.'

'I hope so. I can't imagine even one day without you in my life,' she said honestly, as she held his hand in hers.

'You're never getting rid of me, babe,' he smiled warmly. 'Best friends forever.'

'We really are, aren't we? To think that it's always been just the two of us and neither of us has ever even kissed anyone else...' She hesitated as she remembered that one kiss with Panos. He believed she had thought he was Theo, but she had been in a dream-like state and had been imagining it was him all along, only to be shocked by her desire when her actions became a reality.

'Erm...' Theo wondered if he should admit what happened with Rosie, but that might make things much more complicated.

'Oh yes, except for your regular trysts with Beyonce,' she laughed.

'A man's only human,' he smirked.

'Well, feel free to make the most of her while I'm away.'

'It's weird how you're not jealous,' he said, flinching as he realised he'd said it out loud.

'Of Beyonce?'

'Of knowing I dream about getting up close and personal with someone else.' He was interested to know what she would say, because he didn't feel jealous thinking of her doing the same thing either.

'But it's not real, is it?' she shrugged.

'I suppose not, but it feels real in my head.'

'And do you feel guilty when you wake up?'

'No.'

'There you are then.'

'But is that normal, to enjoy holding and kissing another woman but then not feeling guilty?' He wasn't sure where he was going with this, but he realised it was connected to his half-naked moment with Rosie. That was real and it had made him feel amazing, but though he knew he shouldn't have done it, he didn't feel guilty and he would love it to happen again without it simply being his regular dream scenario.

'Hearing you say it that way, maybe not. I've just thought it's a dream and not worried about it.'

'But if it was real life, obviously you'd be jealous?'

She couldn't answer immediately, which silently marked an unexpected turning point in their relationship.

'Honestly, I should probably say yes, but that wouldn't be my first thought. I would be upset that you would turn to someone else, but that would just make me wonder if you weren't happy enough with me.'

'Which, of course, I am.'

'Glad to hear it,' she replied with a nod, but her thoughts and emotions were still processing. 'It's not that I would feel I wasn't good enough for you, because I've got plenty of self-confidence and I believe in myself, but I'd wonder if someone else could make you happier.'

'You know, I think I understand exactly what you mean. As long as you're happy, that means everything to me. The fact that you want to move away and start a new career doesn't worry me as long as I know you'll be happy, so I guess it must be something which can make you happier than I can, right now.'

'I hadn't thought of it like that,' she admitted. 'It's like I'm leaving you for someone else, but in this case, it's a new job.'

'I think it's probably a new life,' he gulped, understanding so much more about their relationship than they had actually put into words.

'But we can't just make a decision like that so quickly. We've only just begun to talk about the possibility of me doing this.'

'And look where it led us. You want to change jobs just as much as I want to and I don't think we should hold each other back. Who knows what other opportunities will come to us if we give each other the freedom to see where they might take us?'

'But I love you. We can't just abandon each other.'

'We won't be abandoning anything; we'll always be part of each other's lives. You said you can't imagine even one day without me in your life and there doesn't need to be. I meant it when I said best friends forever. I think that is what we will always be and of course, I love you too.' He paused and looked directly at her when he added gently, 'I'm just not sure I'm "in love" with you anymore.'

'Oh,' she said sorrowfully, hanging her head. He gave her a moment to accept what he had said, in the hope that she would realise that she was feeling exactly the same way.

NOVEMBER

The nightclub on the harbour was having an end of season party, which was an annual event enjoyed by most of the workers after all the tour companies had packed up and gone home.

There was plenty of drinking (a good chance to use up all the less-popular alcohol which had been over-ordered) and dancing (to a lively mix of both international and Greek tunes) and lots of laughter (from all the usual farewell speeches after an amazing season of fun and friendship).

Kyriakos, who had been designated as the evening's hottest party animal, was making sure everyone's glasses were always full and had numerous suggestions - of a musical nature - for the handsome DJ who was keeping them entertained.

He reminded Selina of a bee, but instead of buzzing around the flowers for the nectar, he was buzzing around all his friends to make the most of the occasion and to create lots of unforgettable memories that they would be able to recall lovingly in the following years.

'Isn't this fantastic?' he asked as he slid into the seat beside Selina. 'I'm having just the best time ever!'

'I know; it feels good, doesn't it?' she beamed with equal happiness.

'You'd feel even better on that dance floor with me,' he suggested.

'I'm just having a rest, but I'll be up again once I've finished my drink,' she replied hoarsely, after singing and dancing her way through the last six songs without a break. It wasn't something she was used to doing, but under the circumstances it seemed like the perfect time to step outside her comfort zone.

'I'll hold you to that promise. I love dancing to anything, but Vitaly isn't keen unless it's the Greek music. He does have all the moves when he gets going though,' Kyriakos grinned as he bit his lower lip in anticipation.

'He's really special to you, isn't he?'

'He's everything to me, honestly,' he nodded manically. 'I've never felt like this about anyone before.'

'I didn't realise, I thought you were just finding your way and learning more about how you felt by putting yourself out there. It's great if you've met someone who ticks all your boxes,' she said, gently touching his arm as an encouragement.

'Oh, he definitely ticks all my boxes, if you know what I mean,' he laughed openly.

Selina was still often surprised by the free and easy way her friend expressed himself these days. He had always been pleasant and good fun, but seemed restrained and low-key until he began to explore who he really was. She was glad he had discovered exactly what shape he wanted his life to take and even luckier to have found the person who always brought out the best in him.

'Well, make sure you don't let him get away,' she said, her smile faltering at the thought of what she had almost lost.

'No chance. We're going on holiday to Thailand next month and it's going to be really special.'

'Oh yes. I'm sure that will be lovely.' Should she say romantic? She hadn't had the chance to be romantic for a long time, but she remembered how it could feel and wondered if she would ever get that opportunity again.

'No, I mean *really* special. Can I tell you a secret?'

'Of course.' She was reminded that she was very good at keeping secrets.

'I'm going to propose!' he blurted out and then quickly looked around to make sure no one else had heard. The music was so loud that even Selina, sitting right by his side, had only just heard.

'Oh, wow!'

'I know. And if he says yes, there's a place we can get married in the resort before we come home!'

'That's…' Mad? Brilliant? Scary? What?

'It's crazy, is what it is,' he laughed tipsily. 'But crazy-good, not crazy-bad.'

'Yes, well, congratulations.' She couldn't bear to ask the obvious question, but it must have shown on her face.

'But what if he says no? That's what you're thinking, isn't it?' he shrugged, without waiting for a response. 'Then we don't get married. We won't break up over it, but at least he'll know I'm serious about him and ready to make a commitment. If he's not ready, that's fine, but I just want to let him know that I am.'

'But what about your family? They won't be there for your wedding.' That was a difficult thing to imagine for Selina.

'Well, I can hardly get married in church and, to be honest, I really don't know if they would ever be able to attend a same-sex wedding, even if it was mine. I've told them I have a steady boyfriend, and they're coming to terms with that, but it's never going to be the same as if I was romancing a girlfriend towards the altar. It's a difference of opinion we'll have to learn to live with.'

'But that's such a shame. They must know it hurts you, to lack their support.'

'They support me in private and they really don't love me any less, but accepting Vitaly as my husband is going to take a long time. Years probably, even if it happens at all. We'll have to get used to the family simply treating him as my friend for now, so if we marry away from here, no one will have to face that fact and we can all avoid a difficult situation.'

'Yes, I think sometimes it's good to get away from the ties of home, to enjoy life's many possibilities,' she smiled in understanding.

'Absolutely. It's going to be the start of the rest of my life and I can't wait,' he said as he tapped her glass with his and emptied the contents down in one. 'More drinks! More dancing! More fun!' he said, grabbing Selina's hand to lead her to the dance floor.

'More fun!' she echoed, throwing herself into the spirit of the evening and enjoying the way that Theo was cheering her on from the bar to finally give in to his favourite kind of nightlife.

In the middle of the month, Theo found himself alone at the market place one evening, packing up the souvenirs and mementoes which had become such an integral part of his life.

He had debated keeping the stall and trying to incorporate it into his new life, but he was convinced his plans would be more successful if he just concentrated on one thing at a time.

He'd had a couple of offers of interest, so he needed to itemise the pieces which would be included in the sale and list the contact details of all the regular suppliers, along with a few leaflets of companies he'd recently become aware of who had advertised discounts on bulk orders.

He looked around the huge room and recalled many happy times when it had been bustling with interested customers, with colours and smells and noises which were all typical of a wonderfully welcoming arena, full of fun, playfulness and camaraderie. He would be sad not to call this place home anymore, because that was what it had become over the years, until he'd realised that he'd outgrown it and it was time to move on, just as Selina had done.

He looked over to her stall and smiled at the way she had left a small plant beside the till as a welcoming gift for the cousin who was to take her place. She always made sure she took care of everyone and he was proud of how she had protected her parent's feelings when she'd explained why she needed to leave the island for now to explore bigger career possibilities. There had been a few persuasive arguments to tempt her to stay, but she was very determined and when she confirmed that her course would be complete within three years, so that the original wedding date could remain in place, the temporary opportunity to improve her life had been accepted.

He was overcome with emotion as he realised how much he would miss the market and its happy atmosphere, so he quickly called Selina, knowing she would say all the right things.

'It's just so weird to think neither of us will be sitting here, day after day,' he said.

'I know. It's been such a big part of our lives for so long, but there are going to be other things that we haven't even thought of yet. Like, how will we cope without the daily gossip from Billy in the bakery?'

'Oh yeah. I didn't even mind when he made something up on a quiet day; he still kept us entertained.'

'And then Vitaly would read out all the share prices from the newspaper and tell us which food companies were best for investment.'

'That was only when he wasn't having a competition with Kyriakos to see how many cherries they could each fit in their mouths,' he laughed.

'I was going to say he cheated, but they were both as bad as each other,' she recalled.

'I'm definitely going to miss those two. They really made it fun.'

'I know, but we'll keep in touch. No doubt they'll be sending X-rated photos from their first holiday together very soon.' She wondered if there would be any more commemorative photos on the way, but the proposal was still a secret for now.

'As long as they don't include cherries,' he groaned.

'I will miss the caretaker though,' she declared with feeling. 'I always knew that if anything went wrong, he would step in and save the day. It's going to take some time to find someone else who gives that much unconditional support to other workmates.'

'Yes, he was one in a million, that one. He always seemed to have ladders, or a brush, or a spare lightbulb whenever it was needed. I think he might have been a secret magician.'

'Now that would definitely make sense. And I could probably do with a magician now to miraculously fit all the clothes I want to take into my suitcase.'

'Not going well, then?'

'It was going great, while I was trying everything on and deciding which outfits could be used in different ways; the problem is just that there are too many to fit in my case,' she huffed.

'You need a bigger case,' he said seriously, with echoes of one of his most favourite movie lines.

'I think I'm just going to take two and pay for the extra weight. I was hoping to get Leandra to bring stuff out for me when she visits, but I know she'll fill her case with extra make up and shoes anyway, plus she doesn't even sound that keen about making any plans.'

'She'll just want to know if you've booked her into a five-star hotel first, rather than sleeping on the sofa. She'll never change.'

'No, but I'm glad *we* have. I really appreciate how you've supported this move and made us see things from a new perspective. It's good to know you're behind me and that we'll always have each other to rely on.'

'You know you'll never lose me,' he said reassuringly. 'Now, is there any chance you'll be ready when I pick you up for the airport in the morning?'

'Cheeky. That should be me asking you, Mr I love a lie-in!'

'You're worth it,' he said genuinely as he confirmed a time and closed the call.

He finished packing up the stock together with as much information as he could find and then made his way home, where he was organising his own clothes for a much-anticipated trip.

'Hey gorgeous,' he said as Rosie answered his call.

'Hi, hunky Greek guy,' she replied in her usual sexy way.

'Will I need a specific Christmas jumper, like that bloke off Bridget Jones?'

'If you wear a jumper like that, I'll never speak to you again,' she insisted. 'Just bring a few normal ones and then once you get here you can buy a couple of cheap and cheerful chunky ones for when it gets really cold.'

'How cold is it going to get, exactly?'

'Cold enough to have to drink lots of hot chocolate and mulled wine.'

'That doesn't sound too bad. Maybe I should bring some Metaxa, that always warms me up.'

'If you like. You might end up thinking that the sound of mulled wine is actually better than the taste if you've never had it before, so it could be good to have something familiar.'

'Well, I'll never fit all my mum's best cakes and biscuits in my case, so that's not an option. Hopefully I'll enjoy the flavour of Ireland just as much as I enjoy the accent and that can keep me warm instead.'

They both giggled at his insinuation, but with anticipation and excitement rather than amusement.

'Would she bake anything for you specially, if she knew you were coming here?'

'She would be happy to send me off with anything I asked for, if she thought I was just touring Europe with a mate. Now that she thinks I'm going to Thessaloniki, she presumes Selina will take care of me.'

'And Selina's definitely happy to say you're with her, even though you haven't told her where you're really going?'

'She just understands that I need a break away from here to get my head around all the changes. It's better to say nothing than to lie about things and then get caught out trying to explain myself.'

'I don't really like the deception, but I'll agree to however you want to handle it. I'm just looking forward to showing you around Europe and enjoying some of the nightlife along the way.'

'Yes, I think we're really going to have a blast. I can't wait to get there and spend time with you. It'll be like some wild and crazy holiday where we can just let go and do whatever we want without anyone we know judging us for having a good time.'

'It will definitely be fun,' she promised. 'And it's going to be great to get to know each other better, so we can decide if we want to start something new next year.'

'The tour business?' he clarified.

'Yes, at least the tour business,' she giggled, believing that they were still keeping up appearances, even though Selina and his family were not party to their current conversation.

'Well, I'd better get on and move from making a choice of jumpers, to deciding what kind of tops will give me enough room to manoeuvre at a rave.'

Theo once again confirmed his travel dates and closed the call in a strange echo of his previous conversation, which seemed perfectly normal under the circumstances.

He smiled to himself, thinking about how much fun he was going to have with Rosie, with no one else knowing where he would be. It was a freedom which he hadn't known before and it was providing just as much excitement to know that he could do whatever he wanted as it was to think about who he might be doing it with.

The trip to Ireland and the option to visit other countries with Rosie had been arranged as two friends enjoying something they both had in common, but the flirtatious conversations which had ensued had taken the whole idea to another level where anything was possible. She had already revealed how she felt about him and he could no longer deny his attraction to her either. She put fire in his belly and made him feel alive, as though anything could happen, with a high possibility that it probably would.

She knew his situation with Selina, and was prepared to let him have that, without requiring him to choose between them and he wanted her even more because of it. She even knew that the wedding date had been confirmed and was prepared to let that stand as long as they didn't have to discuss the details.

Nothing had been decided about their future, but with Selina following her special dream, he was taking the chance to follow his own and he was sure it included Rosie. They hadn't even kissed yet, apart from that quick, unfulfilled embrace in the sea, but he knew that they would be together soon and be able to explore what their future held as intimately as they would be able to explore each other, over and over.

He knew that any man would be lucky to find a partner who made his life complete and he realised that he was blessed to have found two very different women, who each gave him something that he needed in a decidedly unconventional way.

Selina woke early, throwing on some warm and comfortable clothes, before hurrying to her favourite spot on the island in order to catch her final familiar sunrise. She knew there would be many to enjoy in her new surroundings, but she wanted to take a clear memory of this one with her as something to remind her of home whenever she was feeling lonely.

She headed east along the coastline, almost as though she was rushing to meet the sun personally as it appeared over the horizon. There was a quiet place on the pebbly beach which was protected from road noise and passing pedestrians by an old chicken coop which was no longer in use. She had never quite understood why someone would keep chickens on the beach, but she knew that it dissuaded tourists from gathering there and so it was a wonderfully private place to be while she took a moment to be mindful and watch the daily miracle of sunrise.

Often, she would turn up and sit down straight onto the shiny pebbles, but at this time of year they became quite slimy and slippery, so she placed a small towel there first and wriggled into the ground until she felt comfortable.

The air was crisp and cool, but not cold, and she gazed at the fading stars as the sky above became lighter and lighter. She was grateful that the few clouds which were in evidence were hovering over the castle and not in any position to affect the anticipated performance of daybreak.

The sky itself seemed to alternately take on every hue of one particular colour as the darkness ebbed away and, although Selina couldn't help giggling at the thought that it looked like fifty shades of grey, she was mesmerised by the slow but sure transformation of the colour scheme.

Finally, the palest grey melted into the palest blue and then deeper and deeper as the brightness of the still hidden sunshine began to make its presence felt. She gazed back over the castle and felt as though she could identify every individual stone which made up its construction as the light hit each one at a different angle. Then her eye followed the coast to the nearer location of the marina, where the moored yachts, which had swayed gently while they were unobserved in the darkness, now danced with passion, their masts grabbing any shaft of light they could find and reflecting it out into the awakening neighbourhood like lasers.

She saw a few fishing boats out in the distance and could just make out some of the birds which were trailing them in the hope of striking lucky with a morning snack. Behind them, she saw the lights along the Turkish coast gradually fade and disappear as a more natural brightness welcomed in the day. She turned back to the east to enjoy the first sharp ray of the sun as it peeked over the distant horizon.

Contrary to her knowledge of natural cycles, she still sometimes wondered if, one day, the sun might glimpse over that horizon and decide it would rather stay asleep for a little longer and hesitate to rise. She liked to pretend that it was a living being with thoughts and desires and that it only rose every morning and set every night because it chose to;

like everyone else, it wanted to enjoy the fun of a beach day and then needed a good sleep to recover before the next morning. Obviously, she knew it would always rise, but she preferred to think that it just wanted to spend the day in the same place that she loved, rather than acknowledge that it was on a constant loop of daylight, without any notion of what was happening in the rest of its orbit.

She watched its progress as it grew full and proud, leaving the security of the land to float unhindered in the sky, which was now ablaze with an intense brilliance which made her eyes water, until she realised that her emotions probably had a lot to do with what was happening.

She closed her eyes and tipped her head back to allow the sun to bathe her in its unfailing light and constant hopeful promise so that she would remember the feeling when she was far away and then she allowed her mind to wander, remaining peaceful under its life-giving rays.

She was equally excited and terrified about what lay ahead. She was lucky enough to have the opportunity to take the first steps towards making her dream come true, but she realised it might not be straightforward and that she could fail at any point. She tried not to put too much expectation into her hopes for the coming months, but she knew she would face some challenges with the knowledge that it may take several attempts to succeed, which would cause frustration and doubt. She didn't doubt she was doing the right thing, but she did doubt whether she would be good enough to actually create a business of her own. She was usually very confident, but this was a new thing which she was attempting alone; in spite of all the support from her family and friends, it would be up to her alone to do all the research and take all the risks and to be solely responsible for whether it worked or not.

That was at the forefront of her mind, but she also had to factor in the work she would be doing for Panos as his model and that was something she was even less sure about.

She had enjoyed working with him on the pieces they had created together, but she wondered if it would be quite as easy when they'd be almost in each other's pockets, with her also living in his studio. Would they be able to separate work and play? They had created a good system for working together, but living in the same environment would be completely different. Would they eat together? If so, who would cook? If they kept their arrangement to a work-only relationship, who would she socialise with? She wished she had spoken to Panos about her doubts before agreeing to his initial suggestion, but she had been so excited about the new life she was possibly heading towards, that it didn't seem important. At least, not at that moment.

Now she was full of questions, but she knew Panos could answer most of them quite easily. It was the questions she was asking about herself that she didn't think she wanted to face.

Once she had acknowledged that this move would provide everything she needed, she had started to analyse the details of what it would mean. There were a lot of changes to take on board and she was ready for the physical and mental challenges it would instigate, but something was holding her back and it took a long time to realise the problem was with an emotional hurdle she had to overcome.

When Theo had said that he wasn't in love with her, it had shocked her to the core. They had both loved each other for so long that she could never have imagined those words coming out of his mouth. She was overwhelmed by his generosity in supporting her to follow her dream, but floored by the thought that his feelings had changed towards her.

They had talked a lot over the next few days and were very honest about their whole relationship and she was relieved to find that they still had a future together and the opportunity to create their own businesses, if they spent some time laying the foundations in preparation.

She had gladly agreed to pay the deposit on the original date for the wedding venue and to cover the orders for flowers and food so that the family could relax and let them get on with things for a few years.

Everything was set up to run smoothly and give them the freedom to bring out the best in each other in their new adventures.

That much she had come to terms with.

The problem was that with all the talk about what was important in a relationship and what the differences were between loving someone and being in love, her mind had analysed each word and she had formed doubts about how she had reacted when she kissed Panos.

Some days she convinced herself that she had just been dreaming and had believed herself to be with Theo, so that was fine. It was a mistake and nothing more to worry about. Other days, when she was feeling lucky about where her life was taking her and that she could be anyone she wanted to be, she realised that she had thought about that kiss an awful lot more than she probably should have. She knew that a part of her had known it was Panos she was with, nestled in those sheets with his warm breath on her face and she allowed herself to enjoy the memory. Nothing had really happened, and certainly nothing had been intended, so she didn't feel too guilty about a momentary lack of clarity which had resulted in a meaningless mistake.

Only it wasn't exactly meaningless. Now that she was going to be living in his studio, in a bed he had probably slept in himself, she realised that she really wouldn't be able to stop it happening again, if the situation arose. She couldn't imagine how that scenario could be repeated, but she tried to picture it somehow, finally realising that she was actually working out how she could make it happen. It surprised her, but also thrilled her and that was when she knew she was in trouble.

She was not going to be able to resist Panos if he tried to kiss her, even though she knew he probably wouldn't try that completely out of the blue. She guessed that they would spend time together at work, growing closer as time passed and he would wait for a sign that she wanted more from their friendship. She quite liked that idea, but knew it wasn't fair on Theo. She also wasn't sure if she would be able to resist Panos for the length of time it would take to become familiar with each other and was worried that it might be her who made some kind of pass after too many confidence-boosting glasses of wine.

She thought back to when they had first met in the market and he had been nervously trying to recreate the displays that Old Mr Mylonas had produced for years. She'd immediately noticed how attractive he was, but it was his sweetness and thoughtfulness which had warmed her heart and made her realise that she didn't want to lose him as a friend when the season ended.

There had been a point when she had thought that she had found another Theo who would always be a steadfast support in her life and at first that had comforted her, but recently she'd wondered why she enjoyed the things she did with Panos more than the things she did with her unofficial fiancé.

He seemed to have grown on her during the summer and opened her up to new and exciting opportunities in a way which Theo had never done. She couldn't help hoping that he would have even more new and exciting things to share with her once they began to find their way towards each other. Now that the beautiful sunrise had filled her with hope, she sent a kiss out to the universe to say thank you for everything which lay ahead of her and hurried home to get started on the first day of the next part of her life.

Theo huffed and puffed as he stored Selina's suitcases in the boot.

'Is that your whole wardrobe?' he gasped as he got into the car and set off for the airport.

'Only the bits I'm going to need.'

'So, all of it then,' he laughed.

'Yeah, more or less,' she joined in. 'I don't really know what different kinds of things I'll need for the different occasions so I just brought pretty much one of everything.'

'You'll have to get a trolley through the airport, you'll never manage to steer those in a straight line at the same time.'

'I know, they'll be running away with me.'

'Panos is definitely picking you up at the other end, isn't he?'

'Yes, he's just confirmed the arrival time so he'll be there.' She quickly squashed the bubbly feeling which the thought produced.

'Make sure he takes care of you. I don't want to hear that you've been left on your own, or you don't know how to get around. He'll be getting a mouthful if he lets you down.'

'I know. He said he'll show me around the area where he lives later today, so I'll know where the shops are and the bus stop is apparently pretty close.'

'For the bus to Thessaloniki?'

'Yes, but again, he's going to drive up there to his offices next week and show me the main town so I'll know my way around when I go on my own.'

'Good.'

'You don't have to worry. If I need something he's unaware of, I can easily ask for it, he's not a bad guy,' she smiled, knowing he was probably the best kind of guy she could have hoped to meet.

'I know, it's just... Well, we've always been together and supporting each other, so it's hard to think of you doing things on your own and, for now, only having one person to depend on.'

'But we'll be talking every day, so I can always ask you what to do if I'm stuck.' Although she realised that she wouldn't be able to tell him everything.

'Make sure you do,' he insisted. 'I want to know every detail.'

'OK,' she nodded. He certainly wasn't going to get every detail. 'But you might be too busy enjoying whatever country you're visiting over Christmas.'

'Well, I guess I might be out of range, but I'll get a voicemail that I can answer later.' He pictured his phone beeping while he and Rosie were in the middle of something that couldn't be interrupted and wondered if he would feel guilty.

'Will you be posting pictures?'

'What?' He was still imagining being naked with Rosie and it seemed wrong for Selina to be requesting pictures of it.

'Will you be posting pictures of the places you visit? I suppose if you want to keep it a secret you won't bother, but it might be nice to see some of the local sights and I could guess where you were.'

'Maybe. It's not really a secret as much as unplanned. I'm just going to go wherever something seems to be happening.' He made a mental note to keep separate files for photographs of scenery and ones with Rosie, so that he never posted the wrong one.

'Well, that sounds exciting,' she said, thinking that it actually sounded very chaotic, and exactly like Theo.

'No, you think that sounds mad, to be so unorganised and at the whim of social media. But that's fine, you know me by now and you know I'll have a great time touring around.'

'Yes, I'm sure you will.'

'And you'll have just as much fun discovering everything there is to know about olive oil, while being the muse for the next big Greek artist!' he declared. 'Which is why we're doing this.'

'I know. I'm so glad we got everything sorted out and managed to clear up all those unspoken feelings.'

'Yeah. Can you imagine if we'd kept it all inside and just continued how we were? We'd never know how good it feels to chase the dream.'

'How long do you think it would have taken before we started blaming each other for holding us back in the same routine forever?'

'I can't bear to think about it. Although, I'm really glad we've built something so solid together through all those years,' he said. 'You've made me the man I am today.'

'I know what you mean; I feel the same way. Having your love and support from as far back as I can remember has given me the confidence to believe in myself and reach for something that I wouldn't otherwise have hoped for.'

They paused for a while, enjoying the connection between them and allowing Selina to take in the scenery as they entered the middle part of the island on the approach to the airport.

She double checked her bag for the flight ticket, a few sweets in case her ears popped on landing, a book about growing vegetables (a new obsession), lip balm and phone charger.

'Oh, I don't believe it, I think I've left my sunglasses at home,' she pouted.

'Really?' he replied with a smirk as he parked the car.

'Yes, I know I can buy another pair, but I really love my aviators.'

'Well, why don't you make a wish?'

'Huh?'

'Make a wish that they'll come to you,' he suggested as he got out of the car to retrieve her cases.

'That's just stupid,' she huffed as she gathered her bits and pieces and opened the door, squinting in the sunlight.

'Just do it, for me,' he asked.

'You are mad,' she laughed and closed her eyes to wish. She would miss his funny ways.

'And there you are,' he pointed.

'What?' she asked as she looked behind her.

'No, they're on your head, silly,' he laughed, as he found a trolley and loaded her cases on.

'Oh! You're teasing. Why didn't you just say where they were?'

'Because I wanted you to have a wish come true before we finally said goodbye.'

'I love you so much,' she said, as the emotion caught up with her and she went to give him a hug.

'And you know how much I love you,' he replied, enjoying the embrace.

'Yes, I do. Even if you're not *in love* with me.'

'Especially because I'm not in love with you. Because then you wouldn't have realised that you're not in love with me!'

'And we would have been walking down that aisle and wasting both of our lives,' she shrugged.

'Instead of paying the deposits ourselves so that no one loses out when we say we've grown apart over the year and decided to break up.'

They took a moment to realise how far they had come and knew for sure that they were ready to let each other go in the hope that their private lives would be just as successful as their working lives. They each hoped the other would find someone they could truly be in love with, but it was too soon to discuss that yet; they needed to settle into new routines and create a new working environment before they would be ready to welcome new partners into their conversations. They knew it would happen, but they just needed some time out to get used to all the changes.

One thing that wouldn't change would be their love and support for each other. They promised to speak every day, until they were each confident that the other was sure they were on the right path, and then they would probably switch to messaging and focus more on developing their own lives.

They were still a couple, but the world had not created a suitable description for the kind of relationship they would have going forward. They were a combination of best friends, siblings, supporters and guardian angels. The only thing they wouldn't be was lovers and that gave them the freedom to be ready for whatever, or whoever, came into their lives in the future. Neither of them realised that the other had already found that perfect partner, but it wouldn't be long until they were all one big happy family.

'So,' she said awkwardly, as the moment to leave approached. 'Make sure you speak to Leandra about the guy at the museum who will give you information about private tours there and the free maps of the historical sites.'

'Yes, I will. But you make sure to keep an eye on the availability of land on the outskirts of town. We won't be able to sell your olive oil on our tours, if we don't have a farm to take the tourists to, will we?'

'I'm on it,' she assured him. 'Well…'

'Come on Li, don't get upset. We'll speak to each other every day; you'll probably get sick of hearing my voice when you've got loads of exciting things going on.'

'Never. I will miss you though,' she said as she began to push her luggage away.

'I'll be with you every step of the way,' he assured her. 'Best friends forever.'

'And ever,' she agreed, carrying the hope of the morning sunrise with her.

Thanks for reading this episode of the Aegean Sun series. If you'd like an exclusive FREE short story entitled The Zia Sunset Excursion, simply request it by adding your email address to the message on the contact page of my website: www.stephaniewood.co.uk

As I'm sure you know, word of mouth is crucial for any author to succeed, so if you have enjoyed **Aegean Sun: The Market Place**, please consider leaving a rating or review at Amazon (even if it's only a line or two).

It would make all the difference and I would be very grateful for your support.

Thank you

OTHER BOOKS IN THIS SERIES

ROOM 101
follows the antics of the holidaymakers in that room of
the Aegean Sun hotel

THE AFTER EFFECTS
reveals what happens when some of those
holidaymakers return home

THE DIARIES
of Mark, the rep, who doesn't hide his feelings

ROOM 102
follows some more holidaymakers a year later, some
returning from Room 101

THE OFFICE
reveals what the reps in the office have to deal with

THE WEDDING
shows Kos out of season for a Greek celebration with
visiting Brits

ROOMS AND REVELATIONS
more fun from the holidaymakers and hotel staff
another year later

THE HIGH STREET
diversifies to locals who work in Venizelou Street, off
Eleftheria Square

A PAIR OF SUMMER SHORTS
Two short stories featuring Eleni the cleaner and Athena
the guide

THE AIRPORT
explores the lives and loves of the people passing
through the airport

THE KAFENION
takes a look at the personal lives of visiting customers
and staff at the café

GRACE'S STORY
reveals the truth behind the secret romance discovered
in The Kafenion – spoilers!

THE MARKET PLACE
shows why some of the locals enjoy working at the
most popular place in town

BEACH SHORTS
Offers a collection of short stories featuring excellent
ways to have fun on a beach

OTHER BOOKS BY THIS AUTHOR

CHRISTMAS ON THE CLOSE series:

The First Christmas

Imogen has her own ideas about what makes a perfect Christmas day and she is pulling out all the stops to make it as delightful as a dream. Can Richard solve the problems that threaten to derail the festive season and stop them from turning her dream into a disaster?

The Christmas Cracker

Paul has grown close to Tricia's son and - from the outside - they seem like a content little family, but will Jacob ever treat him like a real dad?

Why is the man who abandoned her seven years earlier now trying to worm his way back into Tricia's life and will she be tempted to give their relationship a second chance?

A Festive Temptation

Patrick is happy to let Joss take the lead and organise his social calendar, without realising that the arrangements are not always mutually beneficial.

When an unscheduled encounter leads to the suggestion of a new experience, Joss has to decide if she is prepared to stretch the rules but would she, in actual fact, be breaking them?

Countdown to Christmas

Recently-retired Ray is at a bit of a loose end and is looking for something rewarding to fill his time so that he can feel useful again.

When her efficient routine is disrupted by Ray's constant need for attention, will Lorraine pander to his desires or make a clean break to get her life back?

Mistletoe Moments

Veronica and Owen are looking forward to a happy Christmas on The Close and, as their fortieth birthdays approach, some significant celebration will be required, but how can Veronica agree to her husband's life-changing request?

Their son, Travis, is due to take some important exams, but will he be able to concentrate when a serious crush derails his schedule?

The Christmas Miracle

When Diane decides to seek closure with a matter from her past, she unexpectedly finds herself on a journey she isn't prepared for.

Her granddaughter, Emma, has all the technical know-how to assist in the search, but is distracted by an intense - and highly unsuitable - romance.

All the books in

the Aegean Sun series

and the

Christmas on The Close series

are available on Kindle

through Amazon

Printed in Great Britain
by Amazon